Praise for ~~~ ~~~~~~~~

(originally published as *The Locklear Letters*)

A BookSense No. 1 Selection

An Amazon Summer "Breakout Book" Selection

A *Village Voice* "Beach Read" Selection

"A writer in the vein of J.D. Salinger."
—*The Richmond Times-Dispatch*

"A quick and enjoyable tour of the lighter, funnier side of dementia."
—*Kirkus Reviews*

"I don't think I've ever laughed this hard! Ever!"
—Pat O'Brien, *Access Hollywood*

"Its air of droll desperation and sweetly uplifting finale are perfect for those sweltering days when tackling anything more substantial would bring up a sweat."
—*The Village Voice*

"Kun's lighthearted humor pokes clever fun at our ongoing obsession with fame and celebrity."
—*Publishers Weekly*

More Books from Michael Kun

More Books from The Sager Group

Mandela was Late: Odd Things & Essays From the Seinfeld Writer Who Coined Yada, Yada and Made Spongeworthy a Compliment
by Peter Mehlman

#MeAsWell, A Novel
by Peter Mehlman

The Orphan's Daughter, A Novel
by Jan Cherubin

Words to Repair the World:
Stories of Life, Humor and Everyday Miracles
by Mike Levine

Miss Havilland, A Novel
by Gay Daly

Revenge of the Donut Boys:
True Stories of Lust, Fame, Survival and Multiple Personality
By Mike Sager

Lifeboat No. 8: Surviving the Titanic
by Elizabeth Kaye

See our entire library at TheSagerGroup.net

Eat Wheaties! has been adapted for a major motion picture starring Tony Hale (*Veep, Arrested Development*), Elisha Cuthbert (*24, Happy Endings*), Paul Walter Hauser (*Da 5 Bloods, Richard Jewell*), Danielle Brooks (*Orange Is The New Black*), Alan Tudyk (*Dodgeball, Firefly*) and Sarah Chalke (*Scrubs, Roseanne*).

For Jon, Gary, Dave, Nick, Emmett, Steve, Reid, Rich,
Bill and Colin

MICHAEL KUN

EAT WHEATIES!

A Wry Novel of Celebrity, Fandom and Breakfast Cereal

This is a work of fiction. It concerns a fictional protagonist whose fictional story includes references to real and famous people who are placed in wholly fictional situations. The reader is advised that while the names may be of real people, the situations in which they are portrayed are entirely fictional and never actually happened. The book also includes references to wholly fictional characters who are not famous and who are described in wholly fictional ways. As to those, any resemblance to actual persons or events is entirely coincidental.

MICHAEL KUN

EAT WHEATIES!

A Wry Novel of Celebrity, Fandom and Breakfast Cereal

THE SAGER GROUP

Artifex Te Adiuva

FOREWORD

A Note About The Movie Based On This Ridiculous Little Book

Writers are the worst.

Actually, for the sake of accuracy, let me correct that: Writers and lawyers are the worst. It's a photo finish, a dead heat.

That said, I'm a writer. And a lawyer.

And trust me, I'm the absolute worst.

There are people who would put their hand on a Bible and swear to that.

There are people who could say that and pass a lie detector test. Of course, lie detector tests aren't 100% accurate, but still.

I'm not going to bore you by detailing about how terrible lawyers are because I have nothing profound to say on that well-trodden subject. Here's what I will say, though: if you go to a dinner party and are seated next to a lawyer by the host, get ready for a loooooooooooooooooong night filled with a lot of self-congratulatory horse crap.

Same for writers, now that I think about it. Just different self-congratulatory horse crap.

Unlike lawyers, whose skunky reputation is as well-known as it is well-deserved, people tend to hold writers in high regard, perhaps because of some romantic notion that writers are super-duper sensitive and articulate and have some deeper understanding of the human experience than everyone else.

That's garbage, complete and utter garbage.

Writers are just like you and you and you, except they probably bathe less and complain more.

You see, writers like to complain.

About what?

About *every goddam thing.*

If you're a writer yourself, or if you know a writer, this is not news to you.

And if you have ever dated a writer – or went so far as to god-forbid marry a writer, as my beautiful, dark-haired, gray-eyed wife (now ex-wife) did when she wasn't thinking straight – may God bless you for your sacrifice. My beautiful, dark-haired, gray-eyed wife (now ex-wife) knows all about how writers complain. (If she's reading this, all I can say is, "Hey, sweetheart, thanks for putting up with all of my complaining." I'd also thank her for our perfect daughter and for being a great mother, and for the party she threw for my 50th birthday, but that's not the point I'm trying to make here.)

What do writers complain about the most?

1) Other writers, who don't deserve the acclaim or notoriety or money they get because, you see, any successful writer is typically just a talentless, lucky hack in the mind of every other writer.

2) Publishers, who have rejected the writer's submissions because they apparently wouldn't recognize genius and true creativity if they were hit over the head with a frying pan– unless they actually choose to publish the writer's submission, of course, in which case they never seem to offer enough of an advance to the writer, the cheap bastards.

3) Editors, who are always making unreasonable demands of the writer like, you know, spelling words correctly or using proper grammar or insisting that things actually make sense.

4) Agents, who never seem to return the writer's calls quickly enough and take too large of a percentage of any income the writer might make.

5) Whoever designed the book jacket for the writer's book, which never seems to have the writer's name in large enough letters.

6) Book reviewers, who don't understand the writer.

7) Book buyers, who really don't understand the writer or else the book would be an international bestseller.

8) People who write reviews on Amazon, who really really *really* don't understand the writer – unless they give a book a five-star review, in which case they are insightful, sophisticated, and probably exceptionally good looking, to boot.

9) Movies.

Does that last one surprise you?

Well, let me explain.

Writers complain about movies all the time.

If you ever watch a movie with a writer, be prepared for a long talk afterward (probably over coffee because writers love coffee more than they love their mothers) about how the movie would have been worlds better if he or she had written the script because he or she knows so much more about character development and plot and dialogue and gobbledy-gook like that.

And writers always complain that their own books haven't been optioned for a movie because, well, it's pretty clear that the writer's book would be *perfect* for a movie, probably one with Tom Hanks and Julia Roberts, but Hollywood wouldn't know a good story if it bit them on the rear end, right? Right?

But if their books *are* adapted into movies, then you'd better look out – because that's where the complaining really starts and where it gets seriously unpleasant.

"They ruined my book!"

"They changed everything!"

"They missed the point completely!"

"I don't know why they even bought the goddam rights to my goddam book if they were going to make *that* goddam piece of crap."

I've heard those very words from friends of mine whose books were adapted for movies, and I've read article after article about other writers who were beyond unhappy with the film adaptations of their books.

Well, they made a movie based on this ridiculous little book, which was originally called *The Locklear Letters*. They're calling the movie *Eat Wheaties!*

Exclamation point at the end.

It's a better title.

It should have been the original title of this ridiculous little book, now that I think of it. Damn.

So now it's the title on the reprint of this ridiculous little book.

So here's what I have to say about the film adaptation of this ridiculous little book: I LOVE IT!

All capital letters, exclamation point at the end.

The entire experience with the movie was a joy (a word I typically only use when talking to my friend Joy or if I'm eating a Mounds bar that someone put a nut on top of), and the finished product is something I can (and will) watch over and over again until the day I die (it will be a heart attack in my office, mark my words) because, in case you weren't paying attention, I LOVE IT!

I'm thrilled to be able to say this, because it was a long and twisted path that led to this movie finally getting made. And there were no guarantees I would love it.

When *The Locklear Letters* was first published back in 2003, before I even met my beautiful, black-haired, gray-eyed wife (now ex-wife) and before our perfect, curly-haired, math whiz of a daughter (Paige) was born, there was some surprising interest in a movie based on the book. I say it was surprising because it's an epistolary novel. I mean, how do you make a movie out of *letters*?

Pretty easily, apparently.

And the names that were bandied about for the lead character (the star-crossed but good-hearted Sid Straw) couldn't help but make me smile. Ben Stiller, Will Ferrell, etc., etc., etc.

Imagine me smiling.

A production company purchased the film option. They were going to make a movie! It was going to be great!

Then nothing happened.

Imagine crickets chirping (chirp-chirp).

Then someone else purchased the option. They were going to make a movie! It was going to be great!

Then nothing happened.

More crickets (chirp-chirp-chirp).

You can repeat this process a few more times, throw in more crickets (chirp-chirp-chirp-chirp-chirp). Eventually, I stopped thinking anyone was going to make a movie based on the book. And I would have been fine with that. Really.

Then one morning I got a phone call at my fancy law office (the one where I will have my heart attack, mark my words). It was from a screenwriter and director I didn't know, a guy named Scott Abramovitch. It seems he was a friend of my friend Evan Shenkman. And, apparently, Evan had sent him a copy of this ridiculous little book years earlier, and Scott had always wanted to adapt it for a movie, but someone else always had the option. He asked me if I'd let him know when the option was available. It was available right then and there. Eventually we had a deal, then there was a draft script that was remarkably true to the book, and then Scott was talking about casting the movie. He needed to find the right person to play Sid Straw. From time to time, Scott would share the name of an actor who might be interested. I won't repeat their names here only because I don't think I was supposed to know about them.

Scott and I became fast friends, meeting for lunch every week or two to talk about baseball and movies and about actors he was thinking of to play Sid. They were funny and memorable lunches, but I must admit that after a time I began to wonder if he'd be able to find the right actor to play Sid Straw. And without that, there could be no movie. And, again, I would have been fine with that. Really. Then one day Scott emailed me at my fancy, heart-attack law office and said, "Tony Hale wants to do it!"

Exclamation point at the end.

Being a fan of *Arrested Development* and *Veep*, I loved Tony Hale, but I had never even thought of him as Sid Straw until the moment Scott sent that email. It was perfect casting. Perfect. (And you'll agree when you see the movie.)

The rest of the casting came together quickly after that (Paul Walter Hauser, Danielle Brooks, Sarah Chalke, Elisha Cuthbert, Alan Tudyk, Kylie Bunbury, David Walton, Robbie Amell, Hayden Szeto, etc., etc.), and soon they were set to start shooting in different locations around Los Angeles, where I happen to live. And that meant my perfect, curly-haired, math whiz of a daughter (Paige) and I could visit the set on evenings and weekends. (By the way, Paige and I both like to paint on weekends, and you can see some of our paintings hanging on the walls in Sid's home in the movie.)

My Hollywood friends warned me that, as the author of the source material, I would be treated like very old trash when I showed up on the set. It couldn't have been further from the truth. Everyone treated me and Paige like royalty, as they say. And we couldn't have had a nicer time just hanging out with the cast and crew, and watching the filming.

A few of my friends flew in from the East Coast to be extras in the movie (Mike Callahan, Mike Andresino, Stan Smith, Dee Drummond). You can see them in the courtroom scene and in the reunion scene. (You can see me, too, if you're interested – I have a non-speaking role as Dr. Katz in the reunion scene. Yes, that's my bald spot you're looking at.)

I could go on and on and on.

And maybe I will if you ever get stuck sitting next to me at a dinner party.

A number of months later, I was able to see an initial cut of the movie. Then, later, a revised cut. Then another revised cut. Then another one.

I've enjoyed every cut of the movie. I really do love what they did. And I'm proud to have my name on it somewhere. If you see that shot where it says, "Based on the novel *The Locklear Letters* by Michael Kun," that's *me*. That's *this* ridiculous little book.

So, to my friend Evan, who put the book in Scott's hands in the first place, I say, "Thank you. It couldn't have happened without you."

To my new friend Scott, who wrote and directed a film I love: "Thank you for making such a fun movie out of this ridiculous little book."

To the producers David Phillips and Dan Webb: "Thank you for all you have done and for treating me and my daughter with such kindness."

To Tony Hale, Paul Walter Hauser, Danielle Brooks, Sarah Chalke, Elisha Cuthbert, Alan Tudyk, Kylie Bunbury, David Watson, Robbie Amell, Hayden Szeto and the rest of the cast: "Thank you for your performances and for being so kind to me, my daughter and my friends who flew in to be extras."

To Phil Miller, Sal Levin, and everyone on the crew who treated us with such kindness: "Thank you for your excellence and for all of your kindness."

To my film agent Jeff Aghassi, who pushed to have this book made into a movie for more than a decade: "Thank you. Now please return my calls more promptly!"

To my new publisher Mike Sager, who I met at an event many years ago because of this ridiculous little book and who wanted to reprint it in connection with the movie: "Thank you."

To my beautiful, black-haired, gray-eyed wife (now ex-wife) and our perfect, curly-haired, math whiz of a daughter: "Thank you for putting up with me."

To my mother, my friends, and everyone who had such kind words about the book: "Thank you."

I have no complaints today, none at all.

And that's rare for me.

But tomorrow will be a new day, and I'm sure I'll find something to complain about. I'm guessing it will be about the air conditioning in my office. It's always up way too high.

—Michael Kun

From the Desk of Sid Straw

Dear Heather,

    Can you do me a favor?

    You may or may not remember me. We were classmates at UCLA before you went off to become an actress. See if this rings a bell: I dated your sorority sister, Tracy Swid, for a while sophomore year. Remember her? Brown hair, brown eyes. You and I were in a political science class together, too, if I recall correctly. Professor Katz. He fell asleep once during a lecture. Does that help?

    Anyway, my brother, Tom, is a HUGE fan of yours. Not just "Melrose Place," but your other TV shows, too ("T.J. Hooker." "Dynasty." I don't know why I just listed them—you already know the names of the shows you were on).

    I hate to impose, but Tom's birthday is coming up soon. Would it be possible for you to send me an autographed photograph so I can give it to him for his birthday? It would be the perfect gift for him! (He's married, don't worry.)

    Thanks in advance for your help. I hope all is well with you these days. Maybe I'll see you at the reunion next fall.

    Go Bruins!

    Sincerely,

    Sid Straw

    P.S. You haven't kept in touch with Tracy by any chance, have you? I hadn't thought of her in years, until I started writing this note.

══ Sid Straw ══
2748 Palmeyer Street Apt. 230
Baltimore, Maryland 21201

Dear Heather,

I just put a letter in the mail asking for an autographed picture for my brother's birthday, and it occurred to me that I might not have given you my address. Obviously, I wasn't thinking.

Anyway, my home address is:

Mr. Sid Straw
2748 Palmeyer Street Apt. 230
Baltimore, Maryland 21201

You could also send it to me at my work address, if you prefer:

Mr. Sid Straw
Regional Vice President, Sales and Marketing
Empire Software
29915-C Industrial Parkway
Greenbelt, Maryland 21883
Thanks again.
Go Bruins!
Sincerely,
Sid Straw

P.S. I'd hate for you to think I was trying to impress you by including "Regional Vice President" in my business address. It's just that you've got to give the guys in the mailroom as much help as possible if you want to get your mail. As it is, half my mail goes to Sam Haller in Development. Only God knows why or how. It's not as if our names rhyme or something!

Dear Heather,

It's been about three or four weeks since I sent a note off to you asking for an autographed picture for my brother's birthday. Unfortunately, I haven't heard from you yet—unless the guys in the mailroom misplaced something. I've checked with them a couple times, and they've assured me that nothing came. Who knows whether I should believe them. Most of my mail ends up being delivered to Sam Haller in Development. Only God knows why or how.

Anyway, I hate to be a nuisance, but Tom's birthday is coming up in about a month. Would it be possible for you to stick an autographed picture in the mail in the next few weeks? From one Bruin to another, I'd owe you a favor.

Thanks, and best wishes.

Your friend,

Sid Straw

P.S. Home address:

Sid Straw

2748 Palmeyer Street Apt. 230

Baltimore, Maryland 21201

Work address:

Regional Vice President, Sales and Marketing

Empire Software

29915-C Industrial Parkway

Greenbelt, MD 21883

Dear Sam,

You haven't received any of my mail lately, have you? I've been expecting a package from a friend in L.A. I'd appreciate it if you could get back to me ASAP.

Thanks,

Sid Straw

From the Desk of Sid Straw

Dear Sam,

No, I wasn't accusing you of anything. It's just that the mailroom has a bad habit of delivering my mail to you.

If the package should happen to come to you, I'd appreciate it if you'd forward it to me.

Thanks,

Sid Straw

From the Desk of Sid Straw

Dear Sam,
      Thanks for forwarding the package.
      Sid

Dear Mr. Riceborough:

Thank you for having your office forward an autographed picture of Heather Locklear to me.

Unfortunately, I'm afraid it's not Heather's autograph at all. It appears to be one produced by a rubber stamp. In fact, if you look closely, you can see the corner of the stamp itself where someone pressed too hard.

I'm returning the photograph to you. I sincerely hope you've been forwarding my letters to Heather, as I've requested. As she will tell you, we are old college friends. I'm sure she'd be happy to sign a picture for my brother, Tom. (His birthday is only a few weeks away now.)

Thank you for your cooperation.

Sincerely,

Sid Straw

From the Desk of Sid Straw

To the Mailroom,

For some reason, much of my mail is being delivered to Sam Haller in Development by mistake. I would appreciate it if you would use more care to ensure that my mail reaches me.

Thank you,

Sid Straw

Regional Vice President, Sales and Marketing

Dear Heather,

How about this—I'll swap you an autographed picture of ME for an autographed picture of YOU?

I've enclosed an autographed picture of me (it was taken at Ocean City last summer—I'm the one on the left). I'm sure you'll want to frame it and put it on your desk!

I'd appreciate it if you could send the autographed picture as soon as possible—Tom's birthday is right around the corner, as they say.

Thanks,
Sid Straw

Dear Mr. Riceborough:

Thank you for forwarding an autographed picture of Heather. It is most appreciated. I'm sure it'll be his favorite birthday present (although he'll have to pretend otherwise in front of his wife!).

Please thank Heather for me when you speak with her next. (Of course, being a gentleman, I'll send her a personal thank-you note.) Also, please ask her if she'll be attending our college reunion. Maybe you could encourage her to go. It wouldn't be the same without her!

Thank you again.

Best wishes,

Sid Straw

Dear Sam,

Thank you for forwarding the package from Frank Riceborough. I'd appreciate it, however, if you wouldn't open packages that are addressed to me.

Thanks again,
Sid

From the Desk of Sid Straw

To the Mailroom:

My mail is still being delivered to Sam Haller. I would appreciate it if you would take steps to correct this immediately.

Thank you,

Sid Straw

Regional Vice President, Sales and Marketing

Dear Heather,

I just wanted to send you a quick note to thank you for forwarding an autographed picture for Tom's birthday. It is a beautiful picture. You still look terrific. In fact, if you don't mind me saying so, you've gotten even prettier since our school days. I mean that sincerely. (Me, I'm not sure anyone would recognize any longer! Less hair, much more weight, as you can tell from the picture I sent you. It looks like I've got an inflatable pool toy under my shirt these days.)

Please thank your agent Frank Riceborough for his help in getting the picture to me. I'm sure it'll be Tom's favorite birthday present (although he'll have to pretend otherwise in front of his wife!).

Again, many thanks.

By the way, I just remembered something you used to do in college that would make me smile. Whenever someone would say "Goodbye" to you, instead of saying "Goodbye," you'd just wave and say, "Eat Wheaties!" Do you remember that? Better yet, do you still DO that? At this moment, I'm imagining you saying that to someone on the set of *Melrose Place*, and I can't help but smile.

Hope all's well with you these days. Take care of yourself.

Eat Wheaties!

Sid Straw

P.S. Have you heard from Tracy Swid lately?

· UCLA REUNION COMMITTEE ·

Dear Classmate:

Believe it or not, our 20-year reunion is coming up this fall. It certainly doesn't seem like it's been 20 years, does it? If you're anything like me, your memories of college are as fresh as if they happened 20 months ago, not 20 years.

The reunion committee has been working hard to organize the events for our homecoming weekend. Of course, the Bruins will be playing football on Saturday. This year, we'll be playing— or, more accurately, we'll be beating—Oregon State. There will be a pregame luncheon for our class at the Pauley Pavilion. The reunion dinner will be held in the main banquet hall at the Los Angeles Hilton. We are still making arrangements for our Sunday brunch.

I am enclosing some information about the events, along with a list of hotels and special room rates. Make sure to pencil the weekend down on your calendar. Better yet, do it in pen!

Looking forward to seeing you this fall.

Go Bruins!

Sincerely,

Sid Straw

Co-Chairperson, Reunion Committee

· UCLA REUNION COMMITTEE ·

Dear Sarah,

As we discussed, I've made the arrangements for all of the reunion events except the Sunday brunch, which you are planning. I have also sent a letter out to all of our classmates.

I appreciate you're very busy, but I think it would be best if we tried to coordinate our efforts better. After all, we are co-chairpersons.

Please call me at your earliest convenience so that we can coordinate our schedules. Let's make this the best reunion ever!

Very truly yours,

Sid Straw

Dear Tom,

A poem for your birthday:

I love you in blue,
I love you in red,
But most of all,
I love you in blue.

Happy birthday! Hope you like your gift!

Love,

Your older (and smarter) brother,

Sid

P.S. Subliminal message: divorce Janet, divorce Janet, divorce Janet, divorce Janet.

P.P.S. Janet, if you read this card, I'm kidding about the P.S. (at least as far as you know).

Dear Heather,

I can't begin to tell you what a hit your autographed picture was at Tom's birthday party last night. (I hope you don't mind, but I decided to "personalize" it for Tom. Over your signature, I had one of the women in Payroll write, "To Tom, I hope you're as cute as your brother!" Her handwriting matched yours perfectly!)

Anyway, we had the party at our parents' house in Towson. I don't know what it's like for you, but it's still very strange for me to go back to my parents' home. On the one hand, it's like nothing's changed: the same wallpaper, the same photographs, the same faux Hawaiian kitchen table my parents bought thirty years ago. On the other hand, everything's different. Everything, including my parents, is smaller now. It's as if God never wants you to see anything in its true size. Does that make sense?

It was just me, my girlfriend Kate, Tom, Janet (his wife—she looks a bit like Cathy Riordan from your old sorority, now that I think of it), our parents (or smaller versions of them), our sister Amy, who flew in from Cincinnati with her fiancé, Will, and a few of Tom's friends—Jim Something, Tony Something-Else, Fred Who-Knows and their wives. We had dinner (my mother is still the worst cook in Maryland—I swear she could burn water), then we had birthday cake and champagne. After we ate, Tom opened his presents. It's amazing how hard it is to find a gift for a 35-year- old—and Tom's presents showed it. Golf balls, a golf book, a CD by someone I've never heard of (but you probably have). Finally, he opened my gift. You could tell he loved it (but he had to pretend otherwise because Janet was right there!). Your inscription (okay, my inscription) got a big laugh.

Again, my thanks. I owe you a favor. Maybe you could use some computer software?

Take care. Looking forward to seeing you at the reunion.

Eat Wheaties!

Sid Straw

Dear Mom,

Thanks for the GREAT meal last night. You're still the best cook in the entire state of Maryland! And thanks, too, for being so nice to Kate. I know you were a bit upset that she didn't eat more of your lasagna, but I think she was just nervous about meeting you for the first time. I assure you that the fact that she started choking when she first took a bite of your lasagna has nothing to do with her opinion of the lasagna, which was FANTASTIC, but probably has more to do with her having an unusually narrow throat, which makes it hard for her to swallow. I'm sure you'll hit it off with her next time.

Tell Dad the book he got for Tom looks like it's very interesting. I'll bet it was Tom's favorite gift!

Thanks again for a lovely dinner.

Love,

Sid

Dear Heather,

I should have mentioned this before, but I'm going to be in Los Angeles for our annual software convention next week. I know you're probably very busy, but if you have a moment it'd be great to get together for a bite to eat or for drinks. I'll be staying at the Courtyard Marriott in Century City. I don't have the number handy, but I'm sure it's listed in the phone book. Give me a call there if you can break free for a while. (Unlike you, who I presume has to use a fake name wherever you go, I'll be registered under my own, God-given name. Hopefully no computer groupies will be hanging out at the hotel, clamoring for my autograph!)

Hope we can get together.

Eat Wheaties!

Sid Straw

Dear Tom,

The P.S. about divorcing Janet was meant to be a joke. In fact, didn't my note specifically SAY that it was a joke?!?!?

Sid

Sid Straw
2748 Palmeyer Street Apt. 230
Baltimore, Maryland 21201

Dear Heather,

A heads-up: Janet, Tom's wife, has accused me of writing the inscription on your autographed picture. I denied it, which is true: I DIDN'T write the inscription; Carole in Payroll did.

Anyway, Janet says she knows someone who knows someone else who has some connection to the agency that represents you. She says she's going to find out if you wrote the inscription or not. I told her she could go right ahead. I don't know if she'll do it or not—in fact, I doubt she will—but I wanted to give you some advance warning. Forewarned is forearmed, as they say. (I think Dwight D. Eisenhower said that. Or maybe it was Popeye. I always get them confused. Which one of them said, "I yam what I yam"?)

In any event, in the unlikely event that Janet Dubose contacts you or your agent—she kept her maiden name, "Dubose," so don't expect a call from "Janet Straw"—I'd appreciate it if you (or your agent) would tell her that yes, you did write the inscription.

I apologize for any inconvenience this might cause you. This whole thing is just so petty and mean of Janet, but that's the way she is. She hasn't liked me since their wedding day (which is a long, long, LONG story involving her sister), and this is just another way to try to embarrass me in front of my family. (Normally, she'll just say, "Sid, this is EXACTLY why no woman will ever marry you," whenever something happens.)

Thanks again.

Best wishes,

Sid Straw

P.S. Oh, yeah, I almost forgot—Eat Wheaties!

P.P.S. Hope to see you at the software convention!

Tom,

    Okay, maybe I WASN'T joking ....
    Sid

• UCLA REUNION COMMITTEE •

Dear Sarah,

I'm afraid you've misconstrued my letter. My point was that there's a lot of work to be done, and I could use some assistance. I appreciate that you're very busy. I assure you that my job as Regional Vice President of Sales and Marketing keeps me quite busy, too. In fact, I'm hopping on a plane to Los Angeles momentarily and will hardly have a moment of free time in the next few weeks.

I hope we can put our differences aside and work together to make this the best reunion ever.

Sincerely,

Sid Straw

P.S. Any luck finding a place for the Sunday brunch?

Dear Kate,

I'm glad we had an opportunity to talk through some of our issues last night. I completely understand how introducing you as my "girlfriend" at my brother's birthday party might make you feel a bit uncomfortable, especially since we "practically work together" and have only "socialized" a couple times. It was a stupid thing for me to say, and I promise not to "take things too fast" or "jump to conclusions" in the future.

Sid

P.S. In case anyone in my family should ever ask, please tell them that you have a very narrow throat which makes it difficult for you to swallow, okay?

2748 Palmeyer Street Apt. 230
Baltimore, Maryland 21201

Dear Heather,

Sorry I didn't get a chance to see you while I was in L.A. for the convention. It ended up that I didn't have much free time anyway. We had to set up our booth on Thursday night, and it ended up that someone forgot to order a banner for the booth. Fortunately, we found an all-night sign shop on Sepulveda Boulevard, and they were able to print up a sign just in time for Friday morning. It's funny watching everyone walk from booth to booth, filling up their shopping bags with whatever knickknacks everyone's giving away: Empire Software pens, IBM keychains, Grasshopper Computers mousepads, etc., etc. It's like Halloween, except everyone is wearing the exact same costume: computer geek.

I did get a chance to take a walk through campus, though. It's still gorgeous. Founder's Rock. Royce Hall. Rolfe Hall. Pauley Pavilion. The Japanese Gardens. I sat on the step in front of Powell Library for an hour or so, and I swear it was as if I'd never left. Can you believe that almost 20 years have passed? It's incredible, isn't it?

Oh, I also stopped by Fatburger. They still make the best burger in the world. Of course, they're not a dollar anymore.

Again, sorry I didn't see you on this trip. I'll see you at the reunion, though.

Eat Wheaties!

Sid Straw

P.S. You haven't heard from Tom's wife yet, have you? Remember, she goes by "Janet Dubose," not "Janet Straw." I'll owe you a favor if you back me up on this one. Thanks.

Dear Heather,

Big scene at dinner last night, and, unfortunately, it involved you.

As background, I met a nice girl through work a few weeks back. She works for one of our clients. Her name is Kate. She is a bit younger than me, but she's very bright and witty (and, not incidentally, very pretty in an Audrey Hepburn type way, if you look closely enough). Well, we had lunch a few times, then dinner, then dinner and a movie... a fairly typical dating progression, I believe. The long and short of it is that I REALLY like this girl, and I mentioned that to Tom. Tom and Janet invited us over for dinner, and Kate was fairly excited about it. When I picked her up, she looked fantastic. White blouse, black skirt. She looked like an angel, Heather, an absolute angel. On the drive over, I realized I was barely paying attention to the road; instead, 1 was thinking, "I think I am going to marry this girl." You know the feeling I'm talking about? The feeling where, suddenly, you're very afraid of dying?

Then we got to Tom and Janet's house. I reintroduced everyone, and we chatted briefly in the foyer before moving to the living room. When we sat down, Janet looked at Kate and said, "Can I get you something to drink, Heather?"

Kate looked puzzled and said, "My name's Kate."

Then Janet said, "Aren't you Heather Locklear? I thought Sid was dating Heather Locklear."

I tried to laugh and change the subject. I said, "Very funny, Janet. Why don't you knock it off?"

Instead of stopping, she said, "I'm sorry, I got confused. Sid, haven't you told your friend about how you used to date Heather Locklear?"

Kate looked at me with an expression I've never seen from her. Let's just say she didn't look like an angel anymore. I tried to explain that I NEVER said I'd dated you, just that I knew you from college and that you'd sent an autographed picture for Tom's birthday. Before I knew it I was explaining how I had dated Tracy Swid, your sorority sister, and how you and I had taken a class together once (Dr. Katz, who fell asleep). The whole conversation was weird, and it created a tension that hung over all of us like a canopy the rest of the evening. I didn't even get a kiss from Kate at the end of the night, which should tell you something.

Heather, I don't know what to do to straighten things out with Kate now. I can tell she's suspicious of me, but for no good reason. She wouldn't even take my call this morning. And not incidentally, I feel like strangling my sister-in-law, which I assure you I WON'T do: believe it or not, it's still illegal to kill someone in the state of Maryland.

Anyway, it is POSSIBLE that Kate may try to call you (or your agent) to confirm what I told her. If she does, PLEASE tell her about your sorority and Tracy Swid and Dr. Katz falling asleep. Please, Heather: I think I'm falling in love with this girl!

Thanks for your help.

Eat Wheaties!

Sid Straw

Flower Land

Dear Kate,
I know someone who stinks you adorable.
Ted

Dear Heather,

Kate hasn't returned any of my phone calls the past three days. I sent her some flowers on Monday (gerber daisies), and she hasn't even called to thank me.

Did she call you? If so, can you tell me what she said?

Thanks.

Eat Wheaties!

Sid Straw

2748 Palmeyer Street Apt. 230
Baltimore, Maryland 21201

Dear Heather,

Please ignore yesterday's note. I called Kate at home last night. Unfortunately, there was a mixup on the note from the florist, and she didn't know the flowers were from me. It also seems she's been very busy at work this week. Anyway, she loved the flowers, or so she says; I guess I have no reason not to believe her. I mean, what woman doesn't love gerber daisies? (Unless, of course, a guy by the name of, let's say, Steve Gerber broke her heart. Or she had a dog named Daisy that got run over by a car. Or, worst of all, if she had a dog named Daisy that got run over by a car...driven by a guy named Steve Gerber!) We're going to try to get together sometime over the weekend.

Sorry to bother you. I hope all is well.

Eat Wheaties!

Sid Straw

P.S. Did Janet ever call you about the autographed picture? I certainly hope she didn't bother you. Unfortunately, it wouldn't be out of character for her.

═══ Sid Straw ═══
2748 Palmeyer Street Apt. 230
Baltimore, Maryland 21201

To Flower Land:

I am writing to you to express my dismay over the flowers I ordered from your shop earlier in the week. You COMPLETELY screwed up the card!

The card was signed "Ted," instead of "Sid," which is my name. I am not now, nor have I ever been, TED! Making matters worse, it was supposed to say, "I know someone who thinks you're adorable." Instead, it said, "I know someone who stinks you adorable." What does that MEAN? It's gibberish! I assume you'll credit my account.

Sincerely,

Sid (not Ted) Straw

Flower Land

Kate,
Sorry you're so busty at work.
I hope these will make your gay.
Sid

Dear Heather,

Not only haven't I seen Kate in two weeks, I've hardly spoken to her at all. I sent her some more flowers (tulips) with a note: "Kate, Sorry you're so busy at work. I hope these will make your day. Sid." She NEVER called to thank me. (I checked with the florist, who confirmed that the flowers in fact were delivered.) I can't begin to tell you how devastated I am by this. I've hardly been able to work all week.

Anyway, a quick question: did Kate call you or your agent? I'd really like to know. It could explain her behavior and help me figure out what to do next.

Thanks,

Sid Straw

Dear Heather,

Please ignore the note I sent yesterday. I called Kate at home last night and she informed me that she thinks she's going to get back together with her old boyfriend.

Oh, well. Back to being single.

Take care of yourself. I'll look forward to seeing you at the reunion.

Eat Wheaties!

Sid Straw

P.S. Have you heard from Tracy Swid? She was a great girl, wasn't she?

2748 Palmeyer Street Apt. 230
Baltimore, Maryland 21201

To Flower Land:

I lost my girlfriend because you couldn't get a simple note straight!!! I will never use your services again unless you do the right thing and credit my account.

Sincerely,

Sid Straw

2748 Palmeyer Street Apt. 230
Baltimore, Maryland 21201

Dear Heather,

Sorry about writing yet another note this week, but I felt I owed it to you to give you another heads up.

I called Kate at work today just to see how she's doing with her old/new boyfriend, and she said she wished I wouldn't call her anymore. I asked if we could still be friends, and she said she didn't think it was such a good idea. When I asked her why, she said, and I quote, "That whole Heather Locklear thing kind of creeped me out." (That, by the way, is an EXACT quote.)

I tried to explain about how I knew you in college, how I dated Tracy Swid, etc., etc., but she didn't believe me. Finally, I said, "Why don't you go ahead and ask her herself," then I gave her the address of the agency that represents you. So you may be getting a note or a call from Kate any day now. I'd appreciate any help you (or your agent) could give me in straightening this mess out. She's an angel, Heather, an absolute angel. I can't stop thinking about her. I don't want to. There's no way in the world that her old boyfriend could be better for her than I am. After all, he broke up with her once, right? Doesn't that mean he doesn't realize how special she is?

Thanks,
Sid Straw
P.S. Eat Wheaties!

Dear Mr. Riceborough:

I have just reviewed your package in which you have returned all (or what appears to be all) of the letters I sent Heather. I can't begin to tell you how disturbed I am by this— or how disturbed I imagine Heather will be when she learns you're withholding mail from a college classmate. Unless I missed something on the nightly news, I don't believe she's in prison. Like any American, she has a constitutional right to receive her mail.

Now, Mr. Riceborough, I am returning my #!*!" letters in this envelope. Please make sure that they're delivered to Heather AS SOON AS POSSIBLE. I hope you will not engage in such unprofessional conduct again.

Sincerely,
Sid Straw

From the Desk of Sid Straw

To the Mailroom,

    Sam Haller and I are NOT the same person!
Please stop delivering my mail to him.
Thank you.
Sincerely,
Sid Straw
Regional Vice President, Sales and Marketing

From the Desk of Sid Straw

Dear Sam,

I appreciate your sense of humor as much as the next person, and I firmly believe that creating a friendly work environment is essential to the success of Empire Software. That said, I am disturbed by the jokes you have been making at my expense since you discovered my correspondence with my college friend Heather Locklear. As a colleague, I ask you to stop making such jokes. They undermine my authority as Regional Vice President, Sales and Marketing.

I'm sure you understand, and I thank you in advance for your cooperation.

Sincerely,

Sid Straw

═══ Sid Straw ═══
2748 Palmeyer Street Apt. 230
Baltimore, Maryland 21201

Dear Heather,

I don't mean to stick my nose where it doesn't belong, but I wanted you to know how unprofessional Frank Riceborough has been. I know I may have had some kind words about him before, but I'd like to retract them. Not only did he open (and, presumably, read) your personal mail, but he also withheld it from you for months before returning it to me. Thank God there wasn't something critical or time-sensitive in one of my letters! What if one of our classmates had fallen ill, for instance, and you hadn't gotten my note? What if it were one of your sorority sisters? Imagine.

In any event, I have returned the letters to Mr. Riceborough via overnight mail and have asked that he deliver them to you promptly. I trust that he has complied with my request. I hope you will deal with him sternly. I know I would if a subordinate were opening, reading and withholding my personal mail.

I hope all is well otherwise.

Eat Wheaties!

Sid Straw

P.S. Mr. Riceborough: Assuming you open and read this letter, I hope you will be decent and professional enough to deliver it to Heather.

Flower Land

Dear Kate,
Still stinking of you.
Ted

Mr. Riceborough:

STOP RETURNING MY LETTERS!

Sincerely,

Sid Straw

2748 Palmeyer Street Apt. 230
Baltimore, Maryland 21201

THIS NOTE IS NOT TO BE READ BY,
OR GIVEN TO, FRANK RICEBOROUGH!

Dear Heather,

I just thought you should know that our friend Mr. Riceborough is still opening, reading and returning the personal letters I've sent you. This is getting ridiculous. I don't normally give unsolicited advice, but you may want to think about taking steps to have his employment terminated.

I hope all is well and that you'll be able to make it to the reunion. It's just a short drive for you!

Eat Wheaties!

Sid Straw

═══ Sid Straw ═══
2748 Palmeyer Street Apt. 230
Baltimore, Maryland 21201

Dear Mr. Riceborough:

Let me put this in language even you can understand:
STOP RETURNING MY GODDAMNED LETTERS, YOU
RAT BASTARD!

Sincerely,

Sid Straw

• UCLA REUNION COMMITTEE •

Dear Sarah,

    I haven't heard from you. Have you had any luck finding a place for Sunday brunch for reunion weekend?

    Let's talk soon.

    Sincerely,

    Sid Straw

Dear Mr. Callahan:

I am in receipt of your letter threatening to obtain a restraining order to ensure that I at all times "maintain a distance of 100 yards from Mr. Frank Riceborough."

Your letter was entirely unnecessary. First, I have no interest in harming Mr. Riceborough. I am not a violent person. In fact, I make annual contributions to Greenpeace.

Second, I LIVE IN BALTIMORE, MARYLAND! As such, I will be maintaining a distance of approximately TWO THOUSAND MILES from Mr. Riceborough.

Third, all of this could have been avoided had Mr. Riceborough performed a relatively simple task—handing my *personal* letters to Heather Locklear, my college classmate. If a dog can deliver a newspaper to its owner, then certainly Mr. Riceborough is capable of delivering a few letters—or could be trained to do it!

In the interest of avoiding any more conflict with Mr. Riceborough, I will direct any future correspondence for Heather (should there in fact be any future correspondence) to your law firm.

Very truly yours,
Sid Straw

To the Mailroom:

This isn't complicated.

Anything addressed to "Sid Straw" should be delivered to "Sid Straw."

Anything addressed to "Sam Haller" should be delivered to "Sam Haller."

It couldn't be any simpler.

Sincerely,

Sid Straw

Regional Vice President, Sales and Marketing

From the Desk of Sid Straw

Dear Sam,

Please stop with the "Mr. Locklear" jokes. I don't appreciate them, and I am sure that Heather and her husband wouldn't either.

Thank you.

Sincerely,

Sid Straw

═══ Sid Straw ═══
2748 Palmeyer Street Apt. 230
Baltimore, Maryland 21201

Dear Mr. Callahan:

I am in receipt of the restraining order you obtained from the Los Angeles County Superior Court.

This is outrageous. I will be meeting with my lawyer later this week to discuss this matter. Before I do, let me say that your conduct in this matter is exactly why everyone— and I mean EVERYONE—hates lawyers.

You'll be hearing from my lawyer shortly.

Very truly yours,

Sid Straw

2748 Palmeyer Street Apt. 230
Baltimore, Maryland 21201

Dear Mr. Buckner:

Thank you for meeting with me last evening to discuss my current legal situation. I was very impressed by your qualifications—I was joking when I said I'd never heard of Yale Law School! However, I am afraid I cannot afford your $320 per hour rate (unless you can resolve this matter for me in eight minutes or less!). Again, I'm joking, of course.

Again, my thanks. I'm sure I'll be able to find legal representation elsewhere.

Sincerely,
Sid Straw

2748 Palmeyer Street Apt. 230
Baltimore, Maryland 21201

Dear Mr. Evans:

Thank you for speaking with me this afternoon about the possibility of providing me legal representation. Unfortunately, I cannot afford your rate of $275 per hour—unless you can resolve this matter in 12 minutes or less! (Of course, I'm joking.)

I'm sure I'll be able to find legal representation elsewhere.

Again, thank you.

Sincerely,

Sid Straw

Sid Straw

2748 Palmeyer Street Apt. 230
Baltimore, Maryland 21201

Dear Ms. Burleson:

Thank you for meeting with me this morning to discuss my current legal situation. I was very impressed by your qualifications, and I assure you that, contrary to my joke, I indeed am familiar with Duke University. Unfortunately, however, I'm afraid I cannot afford your $270-per-hour rate at the present time (unless you can resolve the matter for me in 10 minutes or less!).

Sincerely,
Sid Straw

═══ Sid Straw ═══

2748 Palmeyer Street Apt. 230
Baltimore, Maryland 21201

Dear Mr. Fisk:

Thank you for meeting with me yesterday to discuss my legal situation. While I had never before heard of the John Morris School of Law, I am sure it's a fine institution. Furthermore, your rate of $100 per hour sounds exceedingly reasonable.

I will be in touch with you once I make a decision about who will represent me in this most serious matter.

Sincerely,

Sid Straw

2748 Palmeyer Street Apt. 230
Baltimore, Maryland 21201

Dear Ms. Daugherty:

I wanted to write to follow up on our telephone conversation this morning wherein I inquired about the John Morris School of Law. I have two questions:

1)   Who is John Morris?

2)   What did you mean when you said, "Our school is not accredited at the present time"?

I will look forward to hearing from you soon.

Sincerely,

Sid Straw

Sid Straw ==

2748 Palmeyer Street Apt. 230
Baltimore, Maryland 21201

Dear Mr. Schultz:

Thank you for answering my questions about Mr. Kevin Fisk's status with the Maryland State Bar. I would appreciate it if you would inform me if and when his license to practice law is ever restored.

Sincerely,
Sid Straw

═══ Sid Straw ═══

2748 Palmeyer Street Apt. 230
Baltimore, Maryland 21201

Dear Mr. Fisk:

I am writing to inform you that I have decided not to retain you to assist me with my current legal situation. It does not sound like a particularly complicated matter. As such, I will represent myself.

Sincerely,

Sid Straw

P.S. A "heads-up": the State Bar might be contacting you about practicing law without a license. I sincerely apologize if I said anything I shouldn't have.

From the Desk of Sid Straw

To the Skylar Publishing Company:
    Enclosed is a check for $76.95 for the following items:
    1) *The Layman's Guide to Law*
    2) *Represent Yourself!*
    3) *The Do-It-Yourself Guide to Restraining Orders.*
    The check includes shipping and handling charges.
    Thank you for your prompt attention to this matter.
    Sincerely,
    Sid Straw

Flower Land

I love you very much and wish you all the best on this special day. You are a wonderful woman.
Love,
Ted

═══ Sid Straw ═══
2748 Palmeyer Street Apt. 230
Baltimore, Maryland 21201

Dear Mr. Callahan:

I apologize for the tone of my last letter. I understand that you were merely doing your job and are required to follow your client's wishes, just as I must do in my job.

In any event, you have my word that I will comply with the restraining order and will not venture within 100 yards of Mr. Riceborough. (Of course, since I don't know what he looks like, it's conceivable it could happen by accident—conceivable, but unlikely, since I live 2,000 miles away).

As I indicated in prior correspondence, I will send any letters for Heather to you. I trust you will forward them to her promptly and remind you that they are personal in nature.

Thank you in advance for your cooperation.

Sincerely,

Sid Straw

2748 Palmeyer Street Apt. 230
Baltimore, Maryland 21201

Dear Heather,

I don't know if anyone has informed you about what's been happening with me and Frank Riceborough. I can't even begin to tell you how disturbing (and embarrassing) this has been for me. In 41 years, I've never had a single run-in with the police. I like to think I've led a fairly honest and lawful existence. Now, all of a sudden, someone I've never even met has obtained a restraining order against me from the Los Angeles County Superior Court.

In any event, here's my concern: generally, I have no problem complying with a restraining order requiring me to stay 100 yards away from Mr. Riceborough. After all, he lives in L.A., and I live in Baltimore. However, it's just occurred to me that I'll be out in L.A. for our reunion this fall. (Go Bruins!) I'd appreciate it if you could make sure that Mr. Riceborough stays away from the airport and the UCLA campus that weekend. I'd hate to bump into him accidentally and get thrown in the clinker. I can't imagine I'd survive for five minutes in jail. They'd eat me alive!

In other news, Kate's still not taking my telephone calls. I wonder, did she call you or write to you? If so, I hope you had kind things to say about me, as I certainly do about you.

Looking forward to seeing you at the reunion (assuming the restraining order won't prohibit me from attending!).

Eat Wheaties!
Sid Straw

Sid Straw

2748 Palmeyer Street Apt. 230
Baltimore, Maryland 21201

Dear Mr. Buckner:

I received a bill in the mail in the amount of $320 for "1 hour- Legal advice."

I believe this bill was sent in error. First, I was under the impression that you were providing me with a free consultation. Second, our meeting only lasted for 15 minutes (from 6:20 p.m. to 6:35 p.m., according to the Yale University clock behind your desk).

I am returning the bill herewith.

Sincerely,

Sid Straw

Dear Mr. Buckner:

Contrary to the assertions in your letter, I did NOT agree that I would pay you for your consultation. Furthermore, didn't they teach you how to tell time at Yale? Fifteen minutes is NOT an hour! It never has been, and it never will be!

Your threat to contact a collection agency is ridiculous. You should be ashamed of yourself.

Sincerely,
Sid Straw

═══ Sid Straw ═══
2748 Palmeyer Street Apt. 230
Baltimore, Maryland 21201

To the Skylar Publishing Company:

There appears to have been an error in the order you shipped to me. Instead of sending me the books I requested relating to restraining orders, you sent me the following books, all of which I am returning herewith:

1) *The Young Lovers' Guide to Restraints*
2) *Lusty German Nursing Students Get Tied Up!*
3) *Spank Me! Harder! Harder!*

(The spine on the last of these books was already broken when I received it.)

I ordered the following books:

1) *The Layman's Guide to Law*
2) *Represent Yourself!*
3) *The Do-It-Yourself Guide to Restraining Orders*

I would appreciate it if you would rush them to me as soon as possible as I have a legal matter that requires my immediate attention.

Sincerely,

Sid Straw

From the Desk of Sid Straw

Dear Sam,

Thank you for forwarding the package from Skylar Publishing Company to me. Although I'm disappointed that you opened a package that was clearly addressed to me, I wanted to assure you that I did not order those books. They were sent to me in error, and I am returning them today.

Best wishes,

Sid Straw

From the Desk of Sid Straw

To the Mailroom:

I AM SID STRAW! SAM HALLER IS NOT SID STRAW! SHOULD THAT STATUS CHANGE, I WILl INFORM YOU IMMEDIATELY. IN THE MEANTIME, PLEASE DELIVER MY MAIL TO ME!

Thank you,

Sid Straw

Regional Vice President, Sales and Marketing

Sid Straw

2748 Palmeyer Street Apt. 230
Baltimore, Maryland 21201

To the Luker Collection Agency:

Enclosed is a check for $320.00.

Sincerely,

Sid Straw

P.S. Would you mind giving a message to Mr. Buckner for me? The message is as follows: YALE SUCKS! Thank you.

Dear Mom,

I am very upset to learn that you and Dad had such an ugly argument on Mother's Day, and that he has taken a room at the Holiday Inn. I love you both very much and wish you felt comfortable talking with me about the argument. Perhaps I could help.

Love,

Sid

P.S. On a different, less important note, you've never said a word about the flowers I sent you for Mother's Day. Did you receive them?

2748 Palmeyer Street Apt. 230
Baltimore, Maryland 21201

To the Skylar Publishing Company:

I did NOT read the copy of *Spank Me! Harder! Harder!* that your company erroneously sent me. As I told you in my previous correspondence, the spine was already broken when I received it. If you are looking for a culprit, I suggest you start with the people in your shipping department.

In the meantime, would you kindly send the books for which I have already paid?

Thank you.

Sincerely,

Sid Straw

From the Desk of Sid Straw

Dear Sam,

You didn't happen to read *Spank Me! Harder! Harder!* before forwarding it to me, did you?

The publishing company is refusing to take it back on the grounds that the spine is broken.

Sid

═══ **Sid Straw** ═══

2748 Palmeyer Street Apt. 230
Baltimore, Maryland 21201

To Flower Land:

I can't believe what you just did! This time you delivered flowers to my mother on Mother's Day with a note from "Ted," instead of "Sid." How may times do I have to tell you that my name is SID?! My parents' next-door neighbor is named Ted! You can't imagine the problems you have caused!

If you can't get a simple card right, you shouldn't be in the floral business!

Sincerely,

Sid Straw

=== Sid Straw ===

2748 Palmeyer Street Apt. 230
Baltimore, Maryland 21201

Dad,

I already said I'm sorry about 100 times. Please accept my apology. And please apologize to the next-door neighbors for me again.

Love,

Sid

From the Desk of Sid Straw

Dear Sam,

I was *not* accusing you of being a pervert.
I'm sorry if there was a miscommunication.
Sid

To the Skylar Publishing Company:

I am in receipt of your package in which you forwarded copies of *The Layman's Guide to Law*, *Represent Yourself!*...and *Spank Me! Harder! Harder!*

As I have told you before, I did NOT order the last of these books, nor did I read it when you erroneously sent it to me. THE SPINE WAS ALREADY BROKEN!

Furthermore, I do not understand why you sent this package to my office address, instead of my home address. The package was opened by my assistant Jeanne, who was shocked, to say the least. This has caused me unnecessary embarrassment at work. In fact, I have been asked to meet with the President of the Company tomorrow to discuss this matter.

Please be advised that I will never do business with your company again.

Sincerely,

Sid Straw

From the Desk of Sid Straw

Dear Bob,

Thank you for giving me the opportunity to present my version of the unfortunate incident that occurred in the office yesterday. Jeanne has every reason to be upset. I'm just as upset as she is. You've known me for a long time, Bob, and you know how hard-working and dedicated I am. I'm in early every day, I hardly ever take a vacation, I don't make long-distance calls or use the company's e-mail system for personal matters, I don't waste hours telling jokes in the coffee room like some of our colleagues do. I am as committed as ever to making Empire Software #1!

You have my word as a gentleman and a colleague that I did not order a copy of *Spank Me! Harder! Harder!*, nor have I ever had pornographic materials sent to the office. It was sent to me in error.

I will apologize to Jeanne, as you suggested. Furthermore, if you will return the book to me, I will send it back to Skylar Publishing with a very stern note.

Thank you for your understanding.

Sincerely,

Sid

From the Desk of Sid Straw

Dear Jeanne,

I just wanted to write a short note to apologize for the unusual and upsetting incident in the office the other day. I assure you that I did not order a copy of *Spank Me! Harder! Harder!* It was sent to me in error. I am just as disturbed as you are, and I have already sent a stern note to the publisher about its error and the ruckus it has caused.

I hope we can return to work as normal.

Sincerely,

Sid

From the Desk of Sid Straw

To the Mailroom,

Thank you for finally delivering my mail to me, instead of Sam Haller.

Sid Straw

Regional Vice President, Sales and Marketing

• UCLA REUNION COMMITTEE •

Dear Sarah,
  Any progress on finding a spot for the reunion brunch?
  Sid

Flower Land

Mom,
Flower Land has kindly agreed to
send you this bouquet to apologize
for the mix-up with the note attached
to your Mother's Day flowers.
I hope you enjoy them.
I'm sorry to have ruined Mother's Day.
Love,
Sid

From the Desk of Sid Straw

Dear Bob,

It's been approximately a week, and you still have not returned the copy of *Spank Me! Harder! Harder!* that was sent to me in error. I would appreciate it if you would return it to me so I can return it to the publisher and try to get a refund.

Thanks,

Sid

From the Desk of Sid Straw

Dear Bob,

I was disappointed to hear that you have apparently lost the copy of *Spank Me! Harder! Harder!* that I was planning to return to the publisher for a refund. Would it be possible to reimburse me from petty cash?

Thanks,
Sid

Dear Kate,

Just a quick note to let you know I was thinking of you.

How are things with you and your boyfriend? Hope you have a nice holiday weekend.

Let's talk soon.

Best wishes,

Sid

═══ Sid Straw ═══
2748 Palmeyer Street Apt. 230
Baltimore, Maryland 21201

To the Editor:

I am in receipt of your newsletter, *Spanking Monthly*. I do not know how I got on your mailing list, but I demand that you remove my name from your list immediately. I have no interest in receiving your publication—ESPECIALLY AT WORK!

Sincerely,
Sid Straw

From the Desk of Sid Straw

Dear Jeanne,

My apologies for yesterday's incident. As I explained, I have no idea how or why that unseemly publication was sent to me.

Sincerely,

Sid

Sid Straw

2748 Palmeyer Street Apt. 230
Baltimore, Maryland 21201

To the Editor:

I am in receipt of your publication, *Hot Bottoms Ready for Spanking*. I have no idea how I got on your mailing list, but I demand that you remove my name immediately. I have no interest in receiving your publication—ESPECIALLY AT WORK!

Sincerely,
Sid Straw

From the Desk of Sid Straw

Dear Jeanne,
 Again, my apologies for yesterday's incident.
 Sincerely,
 Sid

From the Desk of Sid Straw

Dear Bob,

I don't know how I got on the mailing list for those publications!

I look forward to talking with you about them soon.

Sincerely,

Sid

From the Desk of Sid Straw

Dear Jeanne,

I am disappointed to hear that you will be transferring to another department, but I'm sure you'll enjoy working with Sam Haller. He's a great guy!

Thanks for all of your help. Good luck!

Sid

From the Desk of Sid Straw

Dear Bob,

Yes, I am familiar with Kate Drew over at General Transport.

She's a great girl. But, no, I haven't been sending her "inappropriate" notes, nor have I been trying to reach her by pretending to be someone named "Ted." I also have no idea what she thinks I was talking about when I said she had a narrow throat since I was clearly referring to my mother's lasagna.

I look forward to discussing this matter with you.

Sincerely,

Sid

Dear Heather,

Have you ever felt like your life was falling apart and you were powerless to stop it? That's the way I feel these days. So many things are happening, and I don't seem to have any control over them.

First, of course, was the restraining order, which you already know about. Then, my parents split up briefly because of a terrible misunderstanding. Then, there was an unfortunate incident at work that I'd rather not discuss. Now, just when I was at peace with those matters, I've been suspended from work for a week, unpaid. Do you remember Kate? It seems Kate's boss called our Company President to complain about me "harassing" her at work. Bob Rich, our President, is generally a good guy, but he doesn't want to lose a big customer. Unfortunately, when he talked with me about this, I said a few things that, in retrospect, I shouldn't have said. Specifically, I said, "How can I be harassing her? I've kissed her, for godssakes!" That was a mistake for two reasons: 1) it was ungentlemanly, and 2) it suggested my interest in Kate was purely sexual, which is not the case at all, as you know. You don't call someone an "angel" if your interest is purely sexual, do you?

The other mistake I made was mentioning the restraining order Mr. Riceborough obtained against me; it seemed to make Bob more convinced that he needed to take some disciplinary action against me. Objectively, I understand that he needed to do something to keep the client's business. Subjectively, 1 don't understand at all. I just keep thinking, "I'm Sid Straw. I was an altar boy and have never been arrested. I'm the Co-Chairperson of our reunion committee. I give money to charity. How can I be suspended from work?" The other thing I keep thinking is, "What does everyone in the office think? How will they treat me when I return?"

You know me, Heather. I'm not a bad guy. I'm not perfect, but I'm not a bad guy.

I hope things are going better for you than they arc for me. If I still have a job and can afford the trip, I'll look for you at the reunion.

Best wishes,
Sid Straw

Sid Straw

2748 Palmeyer Street Apt. 230
Baltimore, Maryland 21201

Heather,

Day 1 of my suspension. So far, it's been entirely uneventful. I slept late, had some coffee and read the paper, then went for a walk. It was a pretty gray day in Baltimore, but what's new? It's always gray here.

I've tried to put together a list of things to focus on. Here's my list so far:

1) Make a commitment to do the best possible work every single day.
2) Eat healthier (I have to admit I eat too much junk food. That stops NOW!).
3) Don't be so picky about who I date.
4) Join a softball league (to stay in shape).
5) Do charity work.
6) Repair my relationship with Tom's wife, Janet. (I have to make her forget about what happened at the wedding. It's been FOUR YEARS ALREADY!)
7) Read more (books, not newspapers or magazines).
8) Spend more time planning the reunion. (We still don't have a place lined up for brunch!)
9) Be more generous.
10) Go to church on Sunday mornings.

Hopefully, I'll be able to stick to my list longer than I normally maintain my New Year's resolutions, Those normally last about five minutes before they go flying out the window like a caged bird released.

The real reason for my letter, however, is to apologize. I don't mean to dump all my problems on you. Heck, we haven't even seen each other in almost two decades. It's just that sometimes the people who knew you when you were younger understand you better than anyone else. So thanks for listening to (or should I say, "reading") my problems.

Eat Wheaties!

Sid Straw

To the Baltimore Union Mission:
    Enclosed please find a check for $25 to help the needy in
Baltimore. You have my admiration and best wishes.
Sincerely,
Sid Straw

Dear Heather,

Day 2 of the suspension.

I picked up a copy of James Joyce's *Ulysses* at the bookstore. I'd been meaning to read it for years and I figured I've got a little time on my hands this week. (Also, if you'll remember, "read more" is item No. 7 on my list of things to do.) Have you read this book? I'm only 3 pages in, and I HAVE NO IDEA WHAT THIS GUY'S TALKING ABOUT! Either the version I bought was the result of some terrible mishap at the printer's, causing the words to be printed in some random order, or this guy's writing is all gibberish. That, or I'm just not sophisticated enough to understand. It's probably that latter, don't you think?

While I was at the bookstore, I also picked up a copy of the new *In Style* magazine because you were on the cover. I hope you take this in the spirit in which it is intended and nothing more, but the picture of you on the cover is absolutely stunning! Really, it's breathtaking. I read the interview, too, and thought it was great. It really seems like you have a perfect life. I couldn't be happier for you! It must be wonderful to have all your dreams come true. In fact, I'll bet every day feels like a dream. Am I right?

Since I had some time on my hands today, I called a few of our old classmates. I talked with Dave Lambert. Do you remember him? He's working on Wall Street these days. He's married and has three kids (two boys, one girl). He sounds very happy. It was great to catch up with him; we probably haven't spoken since the 15th reunion, I may go up to N.Y. to visit him and his family later in the year. It's a quick trip up by plane, train or car. (I'll probably take the train so I can work on the way.) Anyway, he said for me to say hello if I should talk with you. So, "Hello."

I talked with Jim Dailey and Debbie Soriano. They're both doing well, too, and they *swear* they'll be at the reunion. They also asked me to say hello to you. So, "Hello," again.

I tried to track down Tracy Swid on the internet, but couldn't find her anywhere. Maybe you know where she is.

Hope all's well out in sunny California.

Eat Wheaties!

Sid Straw

═══ Sid Straw ═══
2748 Palmeyer Street Apt. 230
Baltimore, Maryland 21201

Dear Heather,

Day 3 of Sid Straw: The Suspension. (Sounds like a movie, doesn't it? Feel free to pitch it to any of your Hollywood producer friends. Of course, I'm more than willing to play the role of the hero, "Sid Straw." I've been rehearsing for a very long time.)

I'm no longer reading *Ulysses*. I'm going to see if the bookstore will let me return it. Why not? God knows the spine's not broken. (If the spine's broken, they won't let you return the book. Trust me.) I'm going to keep the copy of *In Style* magazine, though.

Listen, I need to ask you for a small, minuscule favor. Would you mind not mentioning my suspension (or the allegations of "harassment") (or the restraining order, for that matter) to anyone? I've had a nightmare where I show up at the reunion, and everyone runs away from me. They literally run, like someone's yelled, "Fire!"—and the fire just happens to be wherever I am. They're all running so fast to get away from me—"Look! It's Sid Straw! Run! Run for your life!"— that it resembles a Japanese horror film, the streets flowing with people trying to flee Godzilla. Only YOU can prevent this hideous nightmare from becoming a reality (and ruining our reunion, to boot!). So, this will just be our little secret, okay? Thanks. I knew I could count on you. The girls of Phi Mu sorority are nothing if not reliable.

Take care.

Eat Wheaties!

Sid Straw

Dear Heather,

I was fired. They told me not to return to work when my suspension ends on Monday. How many people do you know who can pinpoint the *exact* moment when their life blew up?

Well, you know one now.

Sid Straw.

Today.

11:15 a.m. on the nose.

KA-BOOM!

Sid Straw

2748 Palmeyer Street Apt. 230
Baltimore, Maryland 21201

Dear Heather,

I'm writing to follow up on the note I sent you yesterday. Would you mind not telling anyone that I was fired? I'm having the same nightmare ... people running ... Godzilla. You know what I mean.

Anyway, sorry yesterday's note was so melodramatic. With this economy, it shouldn't take long for me to find a new job. I'm going to take my time looking and make sure I take the right position. It wouldn't hurt to take things a little easy for a while, either. God knows I could use a rest. Too many late nights at the office.

Eat Wheaties!

Sid Straw

═══ Sid Straw ═══

2748 Palmeyer Street Apt. 230
Baltimore, Maryland 21201

Dear Sam,

Congratulations on your promotion to Regional Vice President, Sales and Marketing! I wish you the best of luck in the position. Please do not hesitate to call if I can answer any questions.

Sincerely,
Sid Straw

· UCLA REUNION COMMITTEE ·

Dear Sarah,

Are you even *trying* to find a place for the reunion brunch? The reunion's only a few months away. We need to make this a *top priority*.

Please get in touch with me as soon as possible.

Sincerely,

Sid

2748 Palmeyer Street Apt. 230
Baltimore, Maryland 21201

Dear Heather,

I wanted to write to you about something disturbing that happened last night. I had dinner with my parents, my brother Tom and his wife Janet last night. It's bad enough that my father is barely talking to me because of a recent mixup, about which I may have already written. What was worse was that, out of the blue, Janet said, "Oh, by the way, Sid, I checked with my friend who knows Heather Locklear's agent, and she says she's never even heard of you." It was a very awkward moment, to say the least: my explaining how you and I went to college together, her insisting that you've never heard of me.

The way I figure it, one of two things happened: either Janet fabricated her whole story just to embarrass me in front of my family, or you honestly don't remember me. I expect (and hope) that it's the former. It would certainly be in character for Janet to do something to try to embarrass me in front of my family: She's still upset about what happened at the wedding. If it's the latter, however, I'm disappointed: Trust me, you know me, Heather. I dated Tracy Swid when you both were in Phi Mu. ("Rattle, rattle, rattle/here come the cattle/Phi Moo!") You and I were in Dr. Katz's poli sci class when he fell asleep. (Someone wrote "Just a little Katz Nap" on the blackboard, remember?) We were on the same intramural volleyball team one semester. I came in second place in the writing competition junior and senior years. I used to write a column for *The Daily Bruin* called "The Bear Facts." (I'm enclosing a couple copies—maybe they'll jog your memory.) Remember?

Anyway, as I've said, I suspect that. Janet only said that you didn't know me to embarrass me. If that was her goal, she achieved it. In spades. She's a horrible, horrible little woman. My brother could've done much better. Unlike me, he was racing to get married. I've always been the tortoise; he's always been the hare. And, as you know, the tortoise always ends up winning. At least in the books I've read. Which do not include *Ulysses*.

I hope all's well.

Eat Wheaties!

Sid Straw

P.S. I have three job interviews next week. One of them is for a Senior V.P., which would actually be a step up from my job at Empire. Keep your fingers crossed for me. Except when you're driving, of course; that could be dangerous!

 THE BEAR FACTS

People Who've Beaten Me Up

BY SID STRAW

My nose has been broken 28 times. I swear that I'm not making that up—28 times. An X-ray of my nasal area looks like kind of a jigsaw puzzle, although my doctor says it reminds him of Hiroshima. (Hiroshima was bombed during World War II. You could look it up.) You see, I used to get into a lot of fights. My dad says it was because I got on people's nerves. (Those weren't his exact words.) My mom said it was because all of the other kids were jealous of me. My mom is a really nice lady. I like her more than my dad. Just don't tell him I said that.

The following is a partial list of people who have done physical damage to me (most of these encounters resulted in my having two cotton balls stuck up my nostrils for an extended period of time):

1. Jeff Hill

Jeff was a good friend of mine in grade school, but he was hyperactive. We used to sit next to each other in Mrs. Converse's social studies course, and when Mrs. Converse would leave the room to readjust her slip, Jeff would belt me over the head with his binder. The one pleasure I took in Jeff's hyperactivity was that he always managed to hurt himself, sometimes worse than he hurt me. Once in the third grade, he broke his arm on a field trip to Newport, R.I.; he broke it trying to punch a boat. He slept over at my house later that week, and when I wouldn't let him read my new Avengers comic book, he bashed me in the face with his cast. I stopped breathing for about a week.

2. Tom Barry
Tom was a neighbor in Maryland. We stopped being friends when he drew a moustache on my Brooks Robinson baseball card. Well, I got really angry and put his best frog under the tire of his mom's car. When he found out, he came over to my house and gave me a really bad Indian rub on my right wrist and tried to shove my turtle in my mouth. Then, he put dog manure in my Orioles batting helmet, but I didn't find out about that until later. ("Manure" is a fancy word for "dog crap," by the way.)

3. Mr. Barry
Mr. Barry was Tom's dad, and he had a really disgusting scar on his face which resembled Lake Champlain. He was really mad because he had *bought* that frog for Tom (I thought everyone got their frogs over at Dubner's Pond). Then he had the nerve to accuse me of setting fire to their mailbox (which I did but wasn't about to admit). Anyhow, he chased me around for a while on his riding lawnmower before he rubbed my face against his stucco house.

4. Doody Gumpis
Doody had the gall to tell me that Nancy O'Hare, my junior high dream girl, had a goldfish-shaped mole on her left breast. Attempting to defend her honor, I got my ribs beat up pretty good. Even worse, Doody ended up taking Nancy to the graduation dance, and, while doing the Latin hustle, he pulled down the top of her dress to reveal the mole. It was shaped more like a wide-mouth bass than a goldfish, though.

5. The Ridgewood Braves basketball team

Sometimes I get pretty excited when I'm in a close game. Sometimes I go a bit overboard. Anyhow, this time we were up by four points with a minute to go, so they fouled me just to stop the clock. Their center grabbed me around the neck and threw me down. So, I jumped up and yelled, "C'mon, I'll take you all on." They accepted. My teammates left to get Gatorade.

6. Scott Hilmer

I told everyone that I went out with Scott's sister when I really didn't. She was so embarrassed that she made her whole family move to another state. Scott got mad because he wanted to stay.

7. Debbie Kastern

I would rather not talk about this one, okay?

8. Mr. Carlson

Mr. Carlson was my homeroom teacher in tenth grade. I once ran into him at a drugstore on a day when I had stayed home even though I was supposed to give an oral report on the history of Dutch housing. He said that he was glad to see that I was feeling better. Then he ran into me with his car.

9. An Unnamed Member of the USC Trojans Marching Band

I made a joke about how the Trojans running back fumbled twice in last month's game against the Bruins. She hit me over the head with her trombone. Which begs the question: WHAT KIND OF GIRL PLAYS THE TROMBONE IN THE FIRST PLACE?"?!

GO BRUINS!

 THE BEAR FACTS

Girls Who Won't Speak to Me
BY SID STRAW

For some reason, I have trouble dealing with girls. I *always* mess up. I always say something or do something completely wrong. Anyway, because of this, there are hordes of girls who refuse to ever speak to me again. This is part of an inexhaustive, multi-volume list I am currently compiling. I'm going to give each volume a Roman numeral to make it look cool.

1. Katie Lynch
I put a salamander down the back of her dress at our First Holy Communion. Not only did it wreck the dress, but it completely ruined the ceremony. She got really embarrassed, because when she first felt the salamander she yelled out, "Holy shit!" in front of the bishop and God and everyone.

2. Cathy Eddard
She worked all day once to make veal cordon bleu for some special dinner that the French Club was having, and my friends and I ate it when she ran next door to borrow something. She ended up bringing Triscuits with Cool Whip on top, and they tossed her out of the club, even though she was the treasurer.

3. My sister Amy
My friend Jeff and I played Frisbee with her brand-new Bobby Sherman album and it broke. We pasted it back together

and it sounded okay to us, but she said we had to buy her a new one. We agreed, but when we got to the store she said she wanted the Tony DeFranco album instead. We said, "No way," that we were only willing to *replace* the album. The case is still in litigation, and I haven't gotten a Christmas present in over 10 years.

4. Anna Van Aker

I once told her that she walked like she was constipated.

5. Nancy Watkins

I forgot to take her home from our junior prom. I mean, it just slipped my mind. Those things happen, you know.

6. Vickie Belvinter

My best friend, Ken, used to call her up every day, listen to her voice, and hang up. Then, like a jerk, he told her that *I* was the one who was doing it all of the time. Anyhow, she ended up going out with him even though I was the one who really liked her, and I swear I never called up to listen to her. Okay, maybe once, but I really didn't enjoy it. I swear.

7. Irene Santello

I hooked her poodle Muffin up to our new electric garage-door while we were talking. I had no idea my dad was coming home early that day. Cross my heart.

8. My Aunt Peg

My brother Tom and I chipped in to get her some electrolysis last Christmas. She wasn't one of our favorite relatives anyhow, so we really didn't care too much when she ran upstairs crying and refused to come down for the turkey and stuffing. Which meant more turkey and stuffing for US!

9. Elaine Villa

I hid in Elaine's gym locker one day hoping to surprise her when she got back from playing field hockey. But I didn't know girls take their showers *before* they go back to their lockers. She was really mad that I saw her naked when we weren't married.

10. Kristin Alderkite

We shared a locker during our sophomore year in high school, and she used to keep a black bra in there. Well, on Halloween I cut some holes in it and used it for a mask. She got really angry because it was her mom's. How weird is that, having your mom's bra in your locker? I mean, imagine if I kept my dad's underwear in my locker.

11. Kate Haskell

Last summer I drove up to New Jersey to visit her. We went out to dinner at a nice Italian restaurant (where I impressed her by asking the waiter what "flavor" wine they stocked) and had some long conversations. Eventually I told her that I thought I loved her. She said she didn't feel the same way, then thanked me for doing her laundry for her all last semester.

12. Terri Manson

I told everyone that her cousin was Charles Manson as a joke, and it ended up that it was *true*. She could have played along when I said it, but she started crying in front of everyone. Then everyone started yelling "Helter Skelter" whenever they saw her, which caused her to develop a really frightening facial twitch. She had to go to therapy. I'm sorry about this one, I swear.

13. Gina Pestler

Tim Pestler, Gina's brother, was one of my good friends in high school (he became my very best friend in the whole world when I found out that Gina was his sister), so I used to hang out at her house a lot. Anyhow, once she and her mom came back earlier than they were supposed to from shopping, and Gina caught me trying on her beige jumpsuit in her bedroom. I think she threw the jumpsuit out after that.

14. Anita Pencilsharpener

I made fun of her name.

15. Tracy Swid

Freshman year, I wrote Tracy a bunch of anonymous notes explaining how beautiful I thought she was. Then I was stupid enough to introduce myself and admit that I had written them. She was mad because she was expecting someone taller. And cuter. And smarter. And funnier. And more exciting. And more athletic. She was not at all impressed when I informed her that I was the best athlete in my whole family. Which was a lie anyway.

GO BRUINS!

2748 Palmeyer Street Apt. 230
Baltimore, Maryland 21201

To the Skylar Publishing Company:

Enclosed please find a check for $24.99 for *Write Like A Pro: A Guide to Writing Success for the Intermediate Writer*. As a former writer, I ask that you use care to make sure you send me the "intermediate" level book, rather than the "beginner" book as I am a published journalist.

Thank you.

Sincerely,

Sid Straw

Sid Straw
2748 Palmeyer Street Apt. 230
Baltimore, Maryland 21201

To the Editor:

As a longtime resident of Maryland (I've lived here my entire life except for college) I have always enjoyed reading *The Sun*. I truly believe that it is the nation's best newspaper. Baltimore is lucky to have such an excellent source for its news.

I do not know how this is normally done, but I wanted to speak with you about becoming a columnist for the newspaper. Although it's been a great many years, I was a columnist for my college newspaper. While attending UCLA, I wrote a column called "The Bear Facts," which students seemed to enjoy immensely. I am attaching a copy of one of the columns as a sample. I hope you will find it entertaining. I believe that your readers would enjoy reading a similar column about Baltimore. Perhaps it could be called something like "Straw on Baltimore," or "The Straw Man." Of course, I would leave the name of the column to you.

I've already given some thought to some of the subjects I could write about: how everyone calls each other "hun" here; how they're *always* doing construction on Interstate 95; how it's hard to look intellectual when you're cracking open a crab with a mallet; how I saw the anchorwoman for the Channel 2 News, Mary Beth Marsden, in the mall last week, and she's even prettier in person than she is on TV; how *no one* goes to Orioles games anymore because the team stinks; how all the kids here play lacrosse, which no one else in the world has even heard of, etc., etc., etc.

I hope you will be as excited about this idea as I am. Please give me a call at your convenience to discuss it. Although I am busy with a number of other projects, I assure you that I would give this column my utmost attention.

Sincerely,
Sid Straw

 **THE BEAR FACTS**

What My Little Brother Eats

BY SID STRAW

My little brother Tom is basically a good kid except for one irritating quirk—he doesn't lose his temper. You can yell at him all you want, and he won't argue back. You can step on his fingers with workboots and pull those little hairs out of his arms and belt him really hard, and he won't fight back. I know—I've tried doing all of those things.

This isn't to say that he doesn't get even, because he does. You see, instead of fighting, Tom waits until whoever has angered him is asleep, absent, or merely unsuspecting. Then he eats one of that person's possessions. It's a perfect crime since, unless an item doesn't sit well in his stomach, there is no evidence.

What follows is a partial list of items that I know for a *fact* that he has consumed. It does not include various household items or personal belongings that have been missing but cannot be traced to him.

Malibu Barbie (and assorted pieces of her wardrobe): My sister Amy said that his new haircut made him look like Helen Reddy. He retaliated by consuming her favorite doll, the one that tans if you stick it under a lamp. The best part of this was that he left one of the severed limbs floating in the bathtub. I swear it was just like *Jaws*, especially when Amy screamed when she found it.

$95.17: After Tom struck out with the bases loaded in a Little League game, my dad smacked him with a comb and made him cut the lawn even though it was dark outside already. Tom waited for him to take a shower, and then ate all of the money that he had left on his bureau. He ate his Exxon card the next day, but only because Dad had the nerve to accuse him of stealing the money.

An autographed picture of Christie Brinkley: Too painful to talk about.

The Altamore's rec room: Kurt Altamore refused to pay Tom for doing his paper route while he was on vacation in Altoona, Pennsylvania. Tom broke into their rec room (that's what you call it when you put wood paneling up in your basement) and ate their ping pong net, part of Mr. Altamore's workbench, a cushion to one of their sofas that's supposed to look like it's Polynesian or something but doesn't look like much of anything now that it's missing a cushion, and a whole bunch of other neat stuff.

A sweater: My sister Amy called him a "big turd" in front of all his friends, so he ate the sweater my parents gave her for her piano recital. He denies doing it, but I caught him throwing up sequins in the middle of the night. No kidding.

Recipes: Mom wouldn't let him shoot off bottle rockets in the backyard. Tom ate her Betty Crocker recipe file. It's all pretty simple. Not that having recipe cards ever helped my mom with her cooking. It was the worst. After 18 years of her cooking, I feel like I'm eating in a five-star restaurant whenever I go to the cafeteria.

A catcher's mitt: Me again. I was playing golf, didn't notice him walk up behind me, and accidentally took a divot out of his left cheek. He was such a baby about the whole thing. I mean, I did replace the divot, just like good golfers do. And he really didn't have to eat my glove since I got grounded for two weeks anyway.

Women's underwear, size 8: We were at Macy's department store with our mother once, and the saleslady called him a "little sickie" because he was walking around the ladies' underwear section. When she turned her back, he started shoving a bunch of those panties with the days of the week written on them into his mouth. He got a Sunday, a Friday, and two Mondays before the saleslady tossed us out.

GO BRUINS!

══ Sid Straw ══

2748 Palmeyer Street Apt. 230
Baltimore, Maryland 21201

Dear Mom,

Thank you again for dinner last night. As always, the meal was terrific.

Sorry that Tom's shrew of a wife ruined the evening for everyone. Again.

Love,

Sid

P.S. I meant to ask you last night, but I forgot. Do you still have all the old copies of my college column in the attic? If so, I may need to borrow them to get some ideas for *The Sun* column I was telling you about. Thanks.

═══ Sid Straw ═══
2748 Palmeyer Street Apt. 230
Baltimore, Maryland 21201

Dear *[InsertName]:*

Thank you for the opportunity to meet with you on *[insert date]* to discuss the *[insert title]* position. I was very impressed by the commitment everyone has to take the company into the future! It's the very type of environment in which I thrive.

If there are any other questions I can answer, please do not hesitate to call.

Sincerely,
Sid Straw

═══ Sid Straw ═══

2748 Palmeyer Street Apt. 230
Baltimore, Maryland 21201

Dear Mr. Callahan:

I have heard nothing from Heather. ARE YOU EVEN
GIVING MY LETTERS TO HER?

Sincerely,

Sid Straw

2748 Palmeyer Street Apt. 230
Baltimore, Maryland 21201

To the Editor:

I wanted to follow up on my recent letter about the column that I'd like to write for *The Sun*.

How about this for an idea: putting the column on the very last page of the Life section and calling it "The Final Straw"? I think most people would enjoy the pun.

I'll look forward to hearing from you soon.

Sincerely,

Sid Straw

══ Sid Straw ══
2748 Palmeyer Street Apt. 230
Baltimore, Maryland 21201

Dear [InsertName]:

I have not heard from you about the [insert title] position for which I interviewed on [insert date]. As you can imagine, I must make a decision about my career shortly. I look forward to hearing from you soon and hope to help take your company into the future!

Sincerely,

Sid Straw

2748 Palmeyer Street Apt. 230
Baltimore, Maryland 21201

Dear Heather,

I am writing to you from the train on the way back home from New York. I went up to spend the weekend with Dave Lambert and his family. (Dave said to say hello. So, "Hello.") His wife Sarah is terrific, and they have three great kids. We had a terrific weekend, sitting out by the pool, cooking on the grill (shish-kebabs, corn-on-the-cob, etc., etc.), watching videos, etc., etc. A terrific time, and it certainly made me forget that I've been out of work, at least for a while. (I didn't tell Dave and Sarah that I'm out of work. I told them I'm working as a "consultant" these days, and they didn't ask for details. Fortunately.)

You know how sometimes it's the little moments that make you smile? Well, I had one of those this weekend. Dave and I took his son Fred to the batting cage on Saturday afternoon. Jon went in the super-slo pitch cage and did pretty well. Then Dave and I decided to try the fast pitch cage. Dave went first, and he did pretty well. Then I went in, and it was amazing—I was hitting everything! Every pitch—Whack! Whack! Whack! I couldn't have missed if I tried. Then I heard Fred say to Dave, "Jeez, Dad, you told me Mr. Straw was good, but you didn't tell me he was this good." That definitely made my day. (Actually, the way things have been going, that made my *month*.)

Dave also told me a very funny story I'd never heard before. It seems that Dave grew up in Meadville, Pennsylvania, which is the same town where the famous actress Sharon Stone grew up. You may have known that if you know her. Anyway, they went to high school together, and apparently Sharon Stone (who Dave said was called "Sharrie" back then) she was babysitting at Dave's friend's house. So Dave and his friend went over there, and Dave started wrestling with her on the living room floor and ended up giving her a "wedgie," which you may recall is what we called it if you tugged on someone's underpants very hard. Sarah says that Dave tells *everyone* about how he gave Sharon Stone a wedgie! And she says he claims that's the reason she wasn't wearing any underwear in that famous scene in the movie *Basic Instinct!* Pretty funny, don't you think?

Well, I hope your weekend was as enjoyable as mine. Looking forward to seeing you at the reunion.

Eat Wheaties!

Sid Straw

P.S. Unless you hear otherwise from me, please remember to tell people at the reunion that I'm a "consultant," okay? Hopefully, I'll have another position by then. In fact, I'm considering a number of opportunities right now, including pursuing a "dream" job—columnist for Baltimore's daily newspaper, *The Sun.*

Sid Straw

2748 Palmeyer Street Apt. 230
Baltimore, Maryland 21201

Dear Dave and Sarah,

Thanks for a terrific weekend. You have great kids and a beautiful home. I had a great time. (And if you're missing anything, I didn't take it! I swear!)

I hope you'll make a trip down to Baltimore sometime soon. It's a great town, and I think you and the kids would enjoy it: the Inner Harbor, the National Aquarium, crabs, the Orioles, etc., etc. Just let me know what weekend you want to come down, and I'll clear my work schedule.

Looking forward to seeing you soon—at the reunion, at the very latest.

Again, my thanks.

Best wishes,

Sid

P.S. And thanks for the great story about giving Sharon Stone a wedgie! It makes me laugh every time I think about it!

To the Skylar Publishing Company:

Why did you send me a book about writing children's stories? I don't have any children, I don't know any children and I have no intention of writing any children's stories! The reason I requested *Write Like A Pro: A Guide to Writing Success for the Intermediate Writer* is that I am trying to refine my skills so I can take on a position as columnist at *The Sun*, Baltimore's daily newspaper. I assure you that very few children read *The Sun*.

Sincerely,

Sid Straw

2748 Palmeyer Street Apt. 230
Baltimore, Maryland 21201

To the Editor:

Thank you for your note. I was disappointed to learn that *The Sun* is not looking for a new columnist at this time. I hope you will keep me in mind should an opening arise. And please don't use "The Final Straw" idea that I shared with you as I intend to discuss that with *The New York Times* in short order.

Sincerely,
Sid Straw

Sid Straw

2748 Palmeyer Street Apt. 230
Baltimore, Maryland 21201

Dear Bob:

Thank you for forwarding my mail to my home, along with my severance check.

I appreciate that my employment at Empire Software did not end as pleasantly as I would have hoped. Nevertheless, I trust that you are providing me with a positive reference whenever you are contacted by the software companies who are interested in my services. It would be the professional thing to do.

Sincerely,
Sid Straw

═══ Sid Straw ═══
2748 Palmeyer Street Apt. 230
Baltimore, Maryland 21201

To the Editor:

I am in receipt of your newsletter, *Spanking Times*, which was forwarded to me from my former place of business, Empire Software. I have no idea how my name got on your mailing list. In any event, I would appreciate it if you would stop sending the newsletters to my (former) business address.

Sincerely,

Sid Straw

2748 Palmeyer Street Apt. 230
Baltimore, Maryland 21201

To the Baltimore Union Mission:

Enclosed please find a check for $25 to help you with your efforts. The work you do is most admirable, and I only wish I had more funds available at this time so I could send a larger check.

Sincerely,
Sid Straw

═══ Sid Straw ═══
2748 Palmeyer Street Apt. 230
Baltimore, Maryland 21201

To Whom It May Concern:

Enclosed is a check for a one-year subscription to *Sports Illustrated*.

Sincerely,

Sid Straw

═══ **Sid Straw** ═══

2748 Palmeyer Street Apt. 230
Baltimore, Maryland 21201

To Whom It May Concern:

Enclosed is a check for a one-year subscription to *Entertainment Weekly.*

Sincerely,
Sid Straw

Sid Straw

2748 Palmeyer Street Apt. 230
Baltimore, Maryland 21201

To Whom It May Concern:
    Enclosed is a check for a one-year subscription to *People*.
    Sincerely,
    Sid Straw

Sid Straw

2748 Palmeyer Street Apt. 230
Baltimore, Maryland 21201

To Whom It May Concern:
  Enclosed is a check for a one-year subscription to *US*.
  Sincerely,
  Sid Straw

2748 Palmeyer Street Apt. 230
Baltimore, Maryland 21201

Dear Heather,

I AM SO BORED!

I know it'll only be a matter of days before I find a new job, but I'm going stir crazy at home.

Question: what do people who stay at home do all day? If you know the answer to that question, please let me know as soon as possible. In fact, send me the answer by Federal Express

Eat Wheaties!

Sid Straw

══ **Sid Straw** ══
2748 Palmeyer Street Apt. 230
Baltimore, Maryland 21201

To Whom It May Concern:

Enclosed is a check for a one-year subscription to *Playboy*.

Sincerely,
Sid Straw

To Whom It May Concern:

Enclosed is a check for a one-year subscription to *Penthouse.*

Sincerely,
Sid Straw

═══ Sid Straw ═══
2748 Palmeyer Street Apt. 230
Baltimore, Maryland 21201

To Whom It May Concern:

Enclosed is a check for a one-year subscription to *Big Boobs*.

Sincerely,

Sid Straw

═══ Sid Straw ═══

2748 Palmeyer Street Apt. 230
Baltimore, Maryland 21201

To Whom It May Concern:

I am now receiving your newsletter, *Spanking Times*, at my home address.

If you are going to continue to forward it to me, at least put it in a plain brown envelope! Jesus!

Sincerely,

Sid Straw

Dear Heather,

I've been doing a lot of reading while I've been out of work. It's amazing how quickly time passes when you're curled up in bed with a good book or magazine.

A strange thing happened yesterday. I was flipping channels on the TV, and I ran across an episode of your old TV show "T.J. Hooker." I don't normally watch cop shows—it's a little too neat that every crime gets wrapped up in exactly one hour—but I watched anyway. There was a scene where you were on the hood of the car trying to hold on while the crook was speeding off at about 100 miles per hour. What was strange was that I was suddenly very worried. Not for your character, but for you as a person. I have no idea how you do stunts like that, but even though I knew you weren't hurt doing the scene, I couldn't help but worry. It's so odd seeing a girl you went to college with holding on to the hood of a speeding car, regardless of the context.

Hope you're doing well. I'm still looking for work. I know something will turn up soon.

Take care.

Eat Wheaties!

Sid Straw

Dear *[InsertName]:*

I still have not heard from you about the *[insert title]* position. If I do not hear from you within five days, I am afraid I will have no choice but to accept another position.

I look forward to hearing from you soon and hope to have the opportunity to help take your company into the future!

Sincerely,

Sid Straw

═══ Sid Straw ═══
2748 Palmeyer Street Apt. 230
Baltimore, Maryland 21201

Dear Bob:

Has anyone from TCSI, Cosmo Software or New World Software called you for a reference? If so, I trust you are speaking very positively of my contributions to Empire's success.

Sincerely,

Sid Straw

Dear Heather,

I AM INCREDIBLY, PAINFULLY, PRETERNATURALLY BORED!

(I just saw the word "preternaturally" for the first time yesterday in an issue of *Entertainment Weekly*. Seems like a good word, don't you think?)

Eat Wheaties!

Sid Straw

P.S. Sorry if this note smells a bit like paint—I painted my living room and dining room today. They're both blue now, in case you were curious. They were blue before, too, but a different shade.

══ Sid Straw ══

2748 Palmeyer Street Apt. 230
Baltimore, Maryland 21201

To Whom It May Concern:

Enclosed please find a check for $19.95 for the "Super Hits of the 70's" CD, which I saw advertised on television last night. Please send it to the above address.

Sincerely,

Sid Straw

2748 Palmeyer Street Apt. 230
Baltimore, Maryland 21201

To Whom It May Concern:

Enclosed please find a check for $39.95 for the Juice-master II, which I saw advertised on television last night. Please send it, along with the bonus peeler, to the above address.

Sincerely,
Sid Straw

Sid Straw

2748 Palmeyer Street Apt. 230
Baltimore, Maryland 21201

To Whom It May Concern:

Enclosed please find a check for $29.95 for the Tooth So White product I saw advertised on television last night. Please send it to the above address.

Sincerely,

Sid Straw

P.S. I hate to butt in, but technically shouldn't it be called *Teeth* So White instead of *Tooth* So White? Tooth So White suggests that it will only whiten a single tooth. I suspect that most customers are like me in that they're trying to get all of their teeth white, not just one of them. Just a thought.

2748 Palmeyer Street Apt. 230
Baltimore, Maryland 21201

To Whom It May Concern:

Enclosed please find a check for $29.95 for the Bead-Dazzler Belt-Maker, which I saw advertised on television last night. Please send it to the above address.

Sincerely,

Sid Straw

Sid Straw

2748 Palmeyer Street Apt. 230
Baltimore, Maryland 21201

Dear Heather,

Did I mention that I decided to try my hand at writing again? As you may recall, I always wanted to be a writer—hence, "The Bear Facts" in *The Daily Bruin*—so I figured I'd give it a try. I mean, when will I ever have as much free time on my hands as now?

Anyway, I gave some thought to writing a column for *The Sun*, which is Baltimore's daily newspaper. Unfortunately, I was unable to reach an agreement with the editor. So, I've put that aside for now and instead I wrote a little children's story the past couple of days just to try my hand at it. It's called "Fred Smells." ("Fred" is named for Dave Lambert's son.) I'm enclosing a copy. Please let me know what you think. I suppose it would be much better if it had illustrations, but I can't draw to save my life. Feel free to use such words as "brilliant" and "astonishing" (or, even better, "preternaturally brilliant" and "preternaturally astonishing"). Who knows, maybe I'll become the next Dr. Seuss!

I look forward to hearing what you think. I'll be holding my breath (figuratively speaking, not literally).

Eat Wheaties!
Sid Straw

FRED SMELLS!

By Sid Straw

This is a story I have to tell.
It's all about Fred—and how Fred smells!
I can say that because I know it's true.
I've known Fred since he was just one or two.
Since he's my best friend, I don't think he'd mind
If I told you he smells ALL OF THE TIME!
Every minute of every day
Fred SMELLS—that's just his way!
Sometimes he'll say, "My, that smells delightful."
Other times, maybe, "Oh, boy, is that frightful."
It just doesn't matter where my friend goes.
Nothing gets past Fred's sensitive nose.
(And if you don't know what "sensitive" means,
It means Fred can smell things he can't even see!)
He'll tip his head back, put his nose in the air,
And say, "Mom's making popcorn, that is if you care."

Or he'll close his eyes tight and then just give a sniff.
"She's baking us apple pie, just get a whiff."
He can tell right away when his dad cuts the grass.
"It smells kind of wet, but then that will soon pass."
He can tell you when painters are working nearby.
"Paint smells a bit bitter, I can't tell you why."
He can tell when his dog takes a swim in the lake.
"It smells so bad, it could make your nose break!"

(And if YOU have a dog who has been soaking wet,
You'll agree with his statement, I would have to bet.)
To see if my friend was the world's greatest smeller,
We conducted some tests one day in our cellar.

(A "cellar," you see, is a word you can use
For the basement of your house, that is if you choose.)
I had Fred sit down and keep his eyes closed.
Then I put lots of things right under his nose.

Whatever I tried, and with no way of telling,
He guessed everything right, only by smelling!
"That smells soapy, so it must be shampoo."
Of course he was right, that was nothing new.
Next I put a flower right under Fred's nose.
"That smells very pretty, it must be a rose."
I thought a sandwich might make him concerned,
"It smells like grilled cheese that's a little bit burned."

(Which is exactly what your parents might want to mutter,
If you made grilled cheese without enough butter.)
I brought a small bottle into the room.
"That one's so easy—my mother's perfume."
"How about this one?" was what I next said,
And I held something round right next to his head.
"Oh, my, that smells awful, please take it away!
Onions make me cry, what more can I say?"

This went on all day, until almost night,
And Fred kept smelling everything—and smelling it right!
Then later that night as I lay in my bed,
I had an idea—and it involved Fred!

It was how we would win the school science fair,
And I'd only need Fred—just Fred and a chair.
(And a fuzzy wool scarf that I normally wore
In the winter when sledding or going to the store.)

When the science fair started in the school gym,
There were projects fantastic, and projects quite grim.
There were gadgets, volcanoes, displays big and small.
There were 117 projects in all!
And what was first prize for all who had hope?
A brand new electronic microscope!
"Now, ladies and gentlemen," I said at my turn,
"What you'll see next, should you care to learn,

Is something you've never seen, I would suppose.
I present Fred—and I present Fred's nose."
Everyone clapped, though a little surprised,
When I put my wool scarf with flair over Fred's eyes.
Only Fred was sniffling as I tied the blindfold.
He hadn't told me that he'd just caught a cold!
(And if YOU'VE had a cold, then you certainly know,
Your sense of smell is the FIRST thing to go!)

I held, a fresh orange, first thing, up to Fred.
"A glass of milk?" was all that he said.
"This has never happened," I quickly confessed,
"But everyone makes mistakes, I guess."
"Try again, Fred, and don't answer in haste."
"Could it be a tube of my favorite toothpaste?"
I tried something different, I tried chocolate cake.
"Is that our science teacher's newest pet snake?"

I tried some floor cleaner that smells like pine trees.
"If that's pepperoni, I'd like a slice, please!"
Everyone laughed so hard, and they laughed for so long,
Because Fred guessed everything—and guessed it all WRONG!
I wish I could say that we still won first prize,
But my mother has warned me about telling lies.
So I'll tell you the truth, 'cause there's nothing to hide,
I will tell you what happened, and say it with pride,

I will tell you the truth, that there's no real disgrace,
In coming in 117th place!
And even though we didn't win first prize that day,
There's still something true that I will always say.
My friend Fred smells, it just is a fact,
It's the way that he is, and the way that he acts,
And he can smell better than me or than you—
As long as he doesn't have a cold or the flu!

2748 Palmeyer Street Apt. 230
Baltimore, Maryland 21201

Dear Heather,

Have you had a chance to read "Fred Smells" yet?

I'm holding my breath. I'm starting to feel very dizzy and lightheaded (although that could be the turpentine—I'm refinishing the dining room chairs).

Looking forward to hearing from you soon.

Eat Wheaties!

Sid Straw (the new Dr. Seuss!)

P.S. Strange thing happened to me today. I was driving, and a woman pulled out of the Burger King parking lot right in front of me. I honked the horn so she would see me. At the next traffic light, she pulled up beside me and, her mouth full, started screaming at me, "I seen you, you bitch! I seen you, you bitch!" Very disconcerting. Is there anything more embarrassing for a man than to be called a "bitch"? (Don't answer that question; I was being rhetorical.) Worse, is there anything more embarrassing for a WORLD FAMOUS WRITER than to be called a "bitch"? (Again, rhetorical.)

Dear Heather,

I'm going to assume that you didn't think too much of the little story I wrote. That's okay, I've reread it, and it's a piece of garbage. I don't know what I was thinking. I'm not a writer, let alone a children's writer. I'm a computer salesman, not a writer. Dreams can't come true for everyone, can they? I mean, if they did, everyone would be a professional baseball player or a movie star or an astronaut. There would be no one left to pick up the garbage or deliver the mail. Which is not to say there's anything wrong with those jobs, but just that no one *dreams* of doing them. At least not anyone I've ever met.

Sorry for wasting your time.

Eat Wheaties!

Sid Straw

Sid Straw

2748 Palmeyer Street Apt. 230
Baltimore, Maryland 21201

Dear Mr. Spellman:

I received your note and was very sorry to hear about Mr. Callahan's untimely death. I did not know him well, but he seemed like a good man. Please pass my sympathy along to his family and the members of your law firm.

Sincerely yours,

Sid Straw

P.S. I hate to trouble you at a time like this, but when you have a moment, can you check to see whether Mr. Callahan has forwarded my letters to Heather. She and I went to college together (UCLA). Thank you in advance for your assistance, especially during your time of grief.

=== **Sid Straw** ===

2748 Palmeyer Street Apt. 230
Baltimore, Maryland 21201

Dear Heather,

I was very sorry to learn of the sudden death of your attorney, Henry Callahan. He seemed like a very kind man, and I certainly appreciate his efforts in passing my notes along to you.

I will be thinking of you during this sad and difficult time.

Fondly,
Sid Straw

World of Flowers

Dear Mrs. Callahan,
I hope you and your family will be able to enjoy life
after your husband's untimely death.
Best wishes,
Sid Straw

2748 Palmeyer Street Apt. 230
Baltimore, Maryland 21201

Dear Mr. Spellman:

I am in receipt of your recent letter. Here is my response: YES, I AM AWARE THAT MR. RICEBOROUGH OBTAINED A RESTRAINING ORDER AGAINST ME! Seeing as I STILL live in Baltimore, and Mr. Riceborough presumably STILL lives in Los Angeles, he has nothing to worry about.

Now, will you kindly tell me whether Mr. Callahan forwarded my letters to Heather before his untimely death and whether you will do so in the future?

Thank you.

Sincerely,

Sid Straw

Sid Straw

2748 Palmeyer Street Apt. 230
Baltimore, Maryland 21201

Dear Mrs. Callahan:

I received your note in today's mail regarding the floral arrangement I sent to your home. I apologize for the confusion. When Mr. Spellman wrote that, "Mr. Callahan is no longer with us," I assumed he meant that your husband had passed away. I didn't understand that your husband had merely left their firm to join another law firm.

I sincerely apologize for any anguish I may have inadvertently caused. I hope you and Mr. Callahan have many happy and healthy years together.

Sincerely,
Sid Straw

• UCLA REUNION COMMITTEE •

Dear Sarah,

    The reunion is only a few months away, and we still don't have a place for the Sunday brunch. Moreover, you haven't responded to any of my letters. Accordingly, I've taken it upon myself to try to find a place.

    I am disappointed you didn't take your responsibilities as co-chairperson more seriously.

    Sincerely,

    Sid Straw

· UCLA REUNION COMMITTEE ·

Dear *[Insert Name]*,

I am co-chairperson for our UCLA class reunion, which will take place the third weekend in November. We are looking for a location for our class's Sunday brunch. Would you be able to accommodate approximately 2,000 people?

I look forward to hearing from you soon.

Sincerely,

Sid Straw

Co-Chairperson

═══ Sid Straw ═══
2748 Palmeyer Street Apt. 230
Baltimore, Maryland 21201

Dear Mrs. Callahan:

I most certainly was NOT threatening your husband's
life. I have no idea how you could have misconstrued my
note. When I wrote that I hope you and Mr. Callahan have
many happy and healthy years together, I was NOT being
sarcastic, nor was I wishing that anything unpleasant would
befall you or your husband.

Very truly yours,

Sid Straw

2748 Palmeyer Street Apt. 230
Baltimore, Maryland 21201

Dear Mr. and Mrs. Callahan:

NOT ANOTHER RESTRAINING ORDER!

You people are crazy! I live in BALTIMORE. Look at a map, for godssakes—it's nowhere near Los Angeles! I'm closer to Cuba than I am to Los Angeles! It'd take me less time to reach Fidel Castro than to reach you!

I will be placing your restraining order where it belongs— wadded up in a ball in my garbage can!

Sincerely,

Sid Straw

Sid Straw

2748 Palmeyer Street Apt. 230
Baltimore, Maryland 21201

Dear Mr. Callahan:

You have misread my letter. When I wrote that I was closer to Cuba than to Los Angeles, I was speaking *geographically*, not *politically*. I am not now, nor have I ever been, a supporter of Cuba's communist regime.

There was no need for you to forward my note to the Central Intelligence Agency, or to send them copies of the restraining orders you and Mr. Riceborough have obtained.

Sincerely,

Sid Straw

• UCLA REUNION COMMITTEE •

Dear Classmates:

Our reunion is only three months away! Hopefully, life has been as kind to you as it has been to me since my last letter.

The alumni office has just informed me that it has received a tremendous number of responses from our class. It looks like our reunion will be even bigger than the one five years ago!

If you haven't registered yet, I encourage you to do so as soon as possible. I'm enclosing information about the reunion weekend, along with a registration card. We have not yet chosen a location for the Sunday brunch. We will notify you as soon as we do.

Looking forward to seeing everyone this fall.

Sincerely,

Sid Straw

Co-Chairperson, Reunion Committee

Dear Dean Warren:

I am in receipt of your letter regarding Henry Callahan. I am sorry that he chose to contact you. Please rest assured that I was not aware that Mr. Callahan was a graduate of UCLA or that he was one of your fraternity brothers. Presumably, he was not aware that I, too, am a Bruin. Perhaps had we each known that, our relationship would have been more cordial.

In any event, you have my word that there will be no shenanigans at homecoming weekend.

Very truly yours,

Sid Straw

2748 Palmeyer Street Apt. 230
Baltimore, Maryland 21201

Dear Heather,

Is Henry Callahan still representing you? If so, could you possibly arrange for me to speak with him by phone? It seems that there have been a number of miscommunications, which have resulted in his obtaining a temporary restraining order against me. What makes this more troubling is that he is a UCLA alumnus, and he apparently has made several sizable donations to the school. My status on the reunion committee is in jeopardy.

I appreciate your assistance.

Your friend,

Sid Straw

P.S. I have two more job interviews this week. Keep your fingers crossed for me.

Dear Mr. Callahan:

This whole thing has been a terrible, terrible misunderstanding. As Dean Warren hopefully has informed you, I, like you, am a graduate of UCLA. In the Bruin spirit, I hope we can put this behind us and move on with our lives.

Best wishes to you and your family.

Sincerely,

Sid Straw

═ Sid Straw ═

2748 Palmeyer Street Apt. 230
Baltimore, Maryland 21201

Dear *[InsertName]:*

It was a pleasure meeting with you on *[insert date]* to discuss the *[insert title]* position. It sounds like a wonderful opportunity and I think it may well be a perfect fit for me.

I look forward to hearing from you soon.

Sincerely

Sid Straw

═══ Sid Straw ═══
2748 Palmeyer Street Apt. 230
Baltimore, Maryland 21201

Dear Sir or Madam:

I would appreciate it if you would send me information about how to apply for unemployment compensation. I have never been unemployed before and haven't the faintest idea how to proceed.

Thank you for your assistance.

Sincerely,

Sid Straw

$\equiv$ Sid Straw $\equiv$

2748 Palmeyer Street Apt. 230
Baltimore, Maryland 21201

Dear Dean Warren:

At your request, and with a very heavy heart, I hereby resign as Co-Chairperson of the reunion committee.

Sincerely,

Sid Straw

To Whom It May Concern:

While I appreciate that you have sent your latest news-letter to me in a plain brown envelope, the fact that the words *Spanking Times* appear on the address label, along with your logo, defeats the very purpose of the plain brown envelope, doesn't it? And if the logo is supposed to look like someone's buttocks, it looks more like the McDonald's logo. Don't be surprised if you get a restraining order. Apparently they're easy to get!

Sincerely,

Sid Straw

Dear Heather,

After finishing painting my home and refinishing my furniture, I started working on a novel last week, and I'm really excited about it. (I know I said in an earlier letter that I was giving up on my dream of being a writer after sending you that appalling children's story, but then I thought about it a bit more. My dream wasn't to be a children's writer; it was to be a novelist. So I thought I should at least try writing a novel before I threw my hands up and quit.)

The novel's about a guy named Sam Bolander, who is either a world-famous baseball player/astronaut/doctor/poet, or he's just some normal guy in a coma who's *imagining* that he's a world-famous baseball player/astronaut/doctor/poet. Ultimately, he has to choose whether he wants to come out of the coma and resume his normal life, or whether he wants to stay in the coma and live his dream life. I'd tell you which one he chooses if I'd decided already, but I haven't. Anyway, I'm enclosing the first chapter. I hope you'll enjoy it, and I hope you'll let me know what you think of it. (Please keep in mind that it's a first draft. Other than that terrible little story I sent you, I haven't done much writing since *The Daily Bruin*. Unless you count interoffice memos, which you shouldn't.)

Hope all is well with you.

Eat Wheaties!

Sid Straw

P.S. I may not be going to the reunion after all. In fact, I've resigned as Co-Chairperson of the Reunion Committee. It's a long, long, long, long, LONG story, I'm afraid.

INVISIBLE SAM

a novel

by Sid Straw

CHAPTER ONE

June 16 — New York City, New York

The weight of being Sam Bolander could snap your bones. I've heard that said a hundred times, a thousand times, but I don't believe there's any truth to it. Seeing as I'm Sam Bolander, and I have been since I popped out of my mama's womb thirty-some-odd years ago, I should know. I should know better than anyone. I should know, I should know.

During a good part of the year—April to October—I'm employed by the Baltimore Orioles baseball squad as their centerfielder. "Batting third for your Baltimore Orioles," the public address announcer will say in a voice as deep as the ocean where it's blue and smells of fish, "batting third, Sam Bolander," and the faithful will applaud and hoot and some will even shout my nickname, "Boo," in an attempt to inspire me to do something spectacular, to send the ball speeding toward some distant spot in the ballpark, to remind them that in this world there are moments of pure joy and glory and wicked pleasure. My mind is sometimes elsewhere though, thinking, planning, computing, conjuring, speculating, twisting, wandering, cursing, eating, drinking, lusting, falling, swooping, rising, predicting, sleeping, waking, hating, loving. Last evening, at the plate against Tommy Heathrow, the Twins ace lefthander, when I should have been concentrating, when I should have been squeezing the bat handle like a cow's teat, I found myself deep in thought about cancer research.

The cure for cancer, I believe, is hidden somewhere in the oxygen molecule. Oxygen, of course, is the most important element to man's existence, and I believe that somehow it provides the answer to this dread disease, as if the Lord has given us a riddle wherein the answer is found in the question itself. Deprive a man of oxygen, and he'll die as surely as if he'd taken a bullet in the temple; deprive a cancer cell of oxygen ... we shall see.

Tomorrow we play the Yankees.

June 17 — New York City, New York

Cancer research, of course, is a little outside my bailiwick. I'm a gynecologist, for godsakes, not a researcher. A gynecologist and a jazz guitarist and a playwright and an astronaut and a private detective and, as I've said, a ballplayer, but I am not a researcher, no matter how much I might dream I were, no matter how much I might wish and pray, no matter how much I might try to will it to be so.

I'm not the only physician in the major leagues, God knows. The Tigers have one at shortstop—Jim Kleinman, an ear-nose-and-throat man. A heck of a fielder, too. Mack Calvin of the Giants is a rheumatologist. And Bob Desormeau was a pediatrician until he got drilled in the ear with a fastball in the playoffs a few years back. They had to carry him off the field on a stretcher, his eye swollen to the size of a potato and purple like a summer plum. That was a sad story. I don't believe he practices medicine anymore; last I heard, he was playing somewhere in the Mexican Leagues, trying to find his confidence with the earnestness of a heartsick man trying to locate a long-gone lover. Bob Desormeau's search had taken him to Juarez.

Which is where I might end up myself if I don't start paying more attention at the plate. If I don't start concentrating. If I don't start concentrating, concentrating, concentrating. The team needs my bat if we're going to catch the Yanks. The team needs my bat, not a cure for cancer. At least not this season.

We're in a doozy of a pennant race with the Yankees right now. The Yankees and the Blue Jays. The Red Sox looked like they might make a run—they were in first place for the first month of the season—but their pitching collapsed. In one game in May, their pitchers gave up 22 runs. Twenty-two! They've fallen 10 games out of first place. Put pennies on their eyes; they're dead. It's just us, the Yankees and the Blue Jays duking it out for first place.

Before today's game, I bumped into Frosty Jenkins while he was running sprints in the outfield. Frosty is a reserve outfielder for the Yanks these days; he was my roommate one season in the minors when we were playing for the Tulsa Eskimos. I have some wonderful memories of those times. Wonderful, wonderful. Memories that linger like chocolate melting on your tongue.

"Boo!" he shouted when he spotted me, and I couldn't help but yell out "Frosty!" myself. Frosty hugged me to him in a way that might embarrass most men, but did not embarrass me. He slapped me on the shoulder. He patted my cheek. There was a thin coat of new sweat on his face.

"Hey, Boo," he smiled.

"Hey, Frosty."

It was a pleasure to see him, a joy. We were very close in the minors—I even introduced him to his wife, Ginny, whom I'd met at a lecture at the hospital where I was doing my residency—but I'm afraid we've lost touch over the years, as old friends are wont to do when their lives become complicated by their jobs and their families and the space program.

"Hey, I saw you on the moon," he said. He pointed to the sky as if to show me the way. "It was on television."

"Yes."

"How was it up there?"

"Very dry. Very lonely." And it is very lonely there. But the solitude gives a man plenty of time to think and dream. It was there, in a moment of solitude and longing that could not be matched on this planet, that I first came upon the idea about oxygen, about how it could be used in curing cancer.

"Things aren't going too well," Frosty confided in me after a while. "I don't know if you've been reading the papers, but I'm not even hitting my weight these days." In fact, I had seen it in *The New York Times* that morning. His batting average was .184; he weighed about 210 pounds. It seemed he was having a harder time concentrating than I was.

"Are you afraid they're going to release you?"

"That or send me down to the minors. I'm not sure I can survive down there again, Boo. The buses, the cheap motels, the greasy food."

Those were my wonderful memories: the buses, the cheap motels, the greasy food.

"Everything will work out," I assured him, and I meant it. "Just concentrate. And don't jerk your head when you swing. Keep your head down."

That had always been Frosty's problem with the Eskimos: He would lift his head when he swung, anticipating the flight of the ball off the bat, but doing that would cause him to drop his shoulder, not noticeably, but enough to alter the arc of his swing so that the ball would duck under his bat and end up in the catcher's mitt for strike one. Then two. Then three.

"Keep your head down," I told him again, and he smiled that perfect smile of his. That was Frosty: all white teeth and a good heart.

"I'll give it a try."

I extended a hand to him, and he shook it.

"Listen," he said before I could run off to rejoin my teammates, "Ginny is here today." He gestured to the seats behind the third base dugout. Though I squinted in the sun, I couldn't see his wife anywhere. Nevertheless, I gave a hearty wave. Fifty people waved back. Two held up their hands with their middle fingers extended as if they were pointing to the moon.

"Listen," Frosty said, "Ginny has been having some pains in her abdomen from time to time." He touched his own abdomen with his fingertips, just below the "NY" of his beautiful pinstriped uniform, the same uniform worn by the likes of Ruth and Gehrig and Mantle and DiMaggio. "Nothing serious, but I'm worried about her just the same."

"Bring her down to the trainer's room after the game and I'll give her a look."

"Thanks, Boo," he said. "Thanks."

"Anytime," I answered. "Just keep your head down."

Jimmy O'Toole pitched for us today. He's still a kid, just a hair over 22 years of age—he even has blotches of acne on his nose and chin—but you'd hardly have known it from the way he played today. He pitched a masterpiece of a ballgame, keeping the batters off-balance, tripping over their feet as if they were just learning to dance, and it was a pleasure to stand out in centerfield on a summer day and watch those Yankees lunging for curveballs, ducking their heads from fastballs, diving as if to avoid an oncoming bus. The Yanks couldn't touch him, but we couldn't scare up a run ourselves against the Yanks' ace, Stan Picotta. He's an enormous man with a belly that looks like he has 30 copies of *Ulysses* stuffed in his jersey and hanging over his belt like an awning. He tires late in a game though, especially in the summer heat. Though he looked unbeatable for the first six innings, we scored two runs off him in the seventh and knocked him out of the game with two more in the eighth. It looked like we had the game wrapped up, four-to-nothing. But you cannot trust anything in baseball. You cannot trust a thing.

The bottom of the ninth was something to remember and something to forget. It made your heart sing and your stomach rumble and your mind swim, and the whole thing happened with the deliberateness of events that you know you are committing to memory just as they are happening. The first two Yankee batters popped up, and the fans began to head for the exits as if escaping a rainstorm.

O'Toole walked the next batter, then gave up a little single through the hole between shortstop and third base. Just like that, the Yanks had two runners on base; the fans turned in the aisles and returned to their seats. The next batter was Carl Babisch, the Yanks' catcher. O'Toole stepped off the mound, rubbing the ball in his bare hands, squeezing it as if he could make it smaller and harder to hit. But the more he rubbed it, the smaller O'Toole himself became until I could swear that I was watching a little boy stepping back onto the mound, with his shirt untucked and his hair slick with perspiration and one sock dangling.

"You're a bum, O'Toole!" someone yelled from the Yankee dugout.

"Did you wet your diapers, O'Toole?"

"Don't cry, little baby."

O'Toole wiped his forehead with his sleeve, and, his shoulders hunched as if against the cold, I knew he was a goner. Before you could say "Jackie Robinson," Carl Babisch had belted a homer into the leftfield stands. The fans pointed at the ball in flight. They were pointing to the moon again.

There was a great roar from the crowd, too, and it hung in the air as our manager, Hippy Hallyday, walked out to the mound. Hippy's an oldtimer, short on patience, but kind still. He raised an arm to signal for Teddy Houston to come in from the bullpen. O'Toole handed Hippy the ball and walked to the dugout with his head bowed like a mourner. There was no reason to be upset with himself; he'd pitched a heck of a ballgame. But the Yankee fans hollered at him just the same, calling him names that I won't repeat, spitting at him.

We were still one out from a victory, but now our lead was down to one run, and the game was now in Teddy Houston's hands. Houston had been struggling lately. He'd lost games to the Royals and the Twins, so it was a surprise to see Hippy call on him in such a close ballgame. It was an act of faith, I suppose, but Houston had nothing today. His pitches seemed to flutter up to the plate. He gave up a single on the first pitch, then a double to the next batter. Suddenly, the Yanks had runners on second and third, and all they needed was a scratch hit to win the bailgame.

Willie Joe Gursky, the Yanks' little second baseman, was due up. He stood in the on-deck circle, swinging three bats at once, the force nearly toppling him. Finally, he turned his head in response to some comment from the dugout, then dropped his bats to the ground and took a seat on the bench. Frosty Jenkins emerged from the dugout.

"Pinch-hitting for the Yankees," the public address announcer bellowed, "Frosty Jenkins," and the fans hissed and booed and made noises like animals in a zoo as if Frosty were one of us instead of one of them.

If Frosty heard them, I can't say. He stepped into the batter's box, tugged at the bill of his helmet, pawed at the red dirt with his cleats, then shouted something to Teddy Houston; I could see his beautiful white teeth moving. Houston's first pitch nearly struck Frosty in the head. What had Frosty said? What?

The next two pitches were strikes.

"Keep your head down, Frosty," I thought, concentrating on those words. "Keep your head down, Frosty. Down. Down."

I wanted him to make contact, to smack the ball solidly. But I wanted the ball to fall in my glove in the end.

Houston threw the next pitch high and outside for a ball. It was two balls and two strikes. What a ballgame!

"Keep your head down, Frosty." I was concentrating so hard that my jaw was growing sore.

The next pitch was a curveball that started high and dipped like the curve of a woman's back. Frosty slid one foot forward and flicked his bat, his head down, down, down. A cheer rang out, and the crowd jumped to their feet anticipating the moment when the ball would plunk down in the grandstand for a home run, but the ball began to die in flight. Tony Campanella, our right fielder, gave chase. He lowered his head, and chunks of earth flew up from his feet like the dirt from the hooves of a great racehorse. The ball began to sink; it wasn't going to reach the seats after all. From where I was, I could see the wad of muscle in Campanella's shoulders as he pumped his arms. He ran and he ran, and finally he sprung forward, extending his glove, and for a moment, the time it takes to sneeze, it appeared that he would grab the ball, but it struck ground instead, landing in the dirt of the warning track a good two feet beyond his reach. The runners on second and third trotted home, and the Yankees had beaten us five runs to four.

And from my spot in deep centerfield, I could see Frosty smiling as his teammates greeted him liked he'd just returned from the war, slapping his back, rubbing his head like a piece of fruit. He smiled and smiled, his white teeth like piano keys. It was the same smile he wore later, after I examined his wife and told him he was going to be a father.

June 17—Baltimore, Maryland

We flew back to Baltimore late last night. Hardly anyone spoke after the tough loss against the Yanks. Hippy Hallyday sat up front with the coaches, mumbling and cursing. The rest of us boys sat in the back, reading magazines or paperback books, some dozing. At one point, Hubie McCaskey, our backup catcher, took his harmonica out and started to play "Stairway to Heaven." He's a terrific harmonica player, and he knows hundreds of songs by heart. Only no one was in the mood to hear him play tonight. A few of the boys put pillows over their heads. Someone threw a magazine. Then Hippy stood up, pointing a finger toward Hubie like he was a witness in court identifying a murderer.

"One more note," Hippy said, "one more note, and I'll shove that harmonica down your throat."

Only Hubie didn't hear Hippy. His own music had drowned it out. He asked Carl Wilbert, our third baseman, what Hippy had said.

"He asked you if you could play a little louder," Carl said, and when Hubie played the song a little louder it took four of us to hold Hippy back, grabbing him by his arms and legs like we were mugging him.

"I'm going to kill that little blankety-blank," he said, though of course he didn't say "blankety-blank." A single vein stood out on Hippy's forehead like a stretch of rope.

"Hippy, don't," I said. "You'll give yourself a heart attack."

"Let me go, Boo," he said.

"Your blood pressure, Hippy. Your blood pressure."

And he considered the source, I guess, then sat down.

No one made a peep the rest of the flight. I opened up my notebook and began to write a poem for Margie, something to give her when I saw her at the gate. But soon I found myself jotting down some notes about the cure for cancer. Maybe if we could isolate the cancer cells and place them in a vacuum for some extended period of time...and then I was sleeping. A deep, dark sleep in which I had a frightening dream the likes of which I'd never had before. I dreamed that I was Sam Bolander, only I wasn't really Sam Bolander. I wasn't a ballplayer. I wasn't a doctor. The closest I'd ever been to the moon was when I'd gone to the top of the Empire State Building. My name was still Sam Bolander, but I was a computer salesman. And Margie wasn't my wife, but a girl whom I occasionally saw from a distance in the food court of our office building. And I was lying in a hospital bed, all sweaty and dreamy and smelling like rubbing alcohol. And someone was standing over me saying, "Your blood pressure. Your blood pressure."

Sid Straw

2748 Palmeyer Street Apt. 230
Baltimore, Maryland 21201

Dear *[InsertName]:*

I am sending herewith the first chapter of my first novel, *Invisible Sam*. Although it is my first attempt at writing a novel, I have more than a bit of writing experience, having written a popular column while at UCLA called "The Bear Facts."

I hope you will enjoy the first chapter of *Invisible Sam* and that your publishing company would be interested in publishing it.

I look forward to hearing from you soon.

Sincerely,

Sid Straw

2748 Palmeyer Street Apt. 230
Baltimore, Maryland 21201

Dear Heather,

You'll never guess who I ran into at the post office yesterday. Kate. Yes, the very same girl who cost me my job at Empire Software.

We spoke for a couple minutes. She said she was doing fine and that things were going well at work. I get the impression that things may not be going well with her new boyfriend (who you may recall was also her *old* boyfriend), because when I asked about him she got a puzzled look on her face and said, "Who?" as if she doesn't give him a lot of thought. All in all, it was a nice conversation, but awkward. I couldn't tell if she wanted me to ask her out. Not that I would do that anyway. Simply, I can't even imagine ever marrying her now. I mean, can you imagine us getting married and me explaining to our children how we got together: "Well, kids, Mommy and Daddy fell in love just a few months after Mommy got Daddy fired, leaving him alone, broke and unemployed." Not a very romantic story, is it?

Anyway, I hope you're doing well today. I saw you in a commercial for hair coloring on TV last night. (It may have been shampoo, now that I think of it.) You looked terrific! Really, I mean it. You always look so happy!

Hope all's well with you these days.

Take care.

Eat Wheaties!

Sid Straw

P.S. I have *six* job interviews next week.

P.P.S. I hope you haven't wasted any time reading the first chapter of my novel. It's garbage, just like that children's story I sent you! Please throw it out. Immediately.

═══ Sid Straw ═══
2748 Palmeyer Street Apt. 230
Baltimore, Maryland 21201

Dear Agent Friedlander:

This letter is to confirm that I have agreed to your request to meet at CIA headquarters in Washington, D.C., on Thursday at 10:00 a.m. I am sure you will see that this has all been a terrible, terrible misunderstanding. I am a good, honest, law-abiding citizen who poses a threat to no one.

Sincerely,

Sid Straw

Dear Ms. Portino:

I am thrilled to receive your letter offering me the Assistant Vice President of Marketing position. Everyone at New Solutions Software seems terrific, and I truly believe I can help take the company into the future!

Sincerely,

Sid Straw

═══ Sid Straw ═══
2748 Palmeyer Street Apt. 230
Baltimore, Maryland 21201

Dear Sir or Madam:

I will be starting a new job with New Solutions Software on Monday. Accordingly, I will not require unemployment compensation any longer. Thank you for your assistance.

Sincerely,

Sid Straw

═══ Sid Straw ═══
2748 Palmeyer Street Apt. 230
Baltimore, Maryland 21201

Dear Heather,

GREAT NEWS! I got a job offer from New Solutions Software to take over as Assistant Vice President of Marketing. While the title is a bit of a step down for me, financially it is an improvement, especially when you consider stock options. I start next Monday.

Hope things are going well for you, too.

Best wishes,

Sid Straw

P.S. Eat Wheaties!

══ Sid Straw ══
2748 Palmeyer Street Apt. 230
Baltimore, Maryland 21201

To The Baltimore Union Mission:

I wanted to share some of my good fortune with the needy people of Baltimore. Enclosed is a check for $100.

Keep up the good work!

Sincerely,

Sid Straw

═══ Sid Straw ═══
2748 Palmeyer Street Apt. 230
Baltimore, Maryland 21201

Dear *[InsertName]:*

This letter is to advise you that I have accepted a position with New Solutions Software. As such, I would like to remove my name from consideration for the *[insert title]* position.

Thank you for your time. I wish you luck in filling the position.

Sincerely,

Sid Straw

Dear Agent Friedlander:

I enjoyed having the opportunity to meet with you and Agents Johnson, Cuellar, Palmer, Reid, Browner, Stapleton, Linz and Mueller yesterday. As you can tell, I am not a threat to national security or to any individuals. Furthermore, while your records are correct and I did take a class called "The Relevance of Lenin and Marx in Late Twentieth Century America" taught by Dr. Stanley Katz, so did hundreds of other students, few if any of whom are Communists, I suspect. I also am not a Communist. In fact, I only took the class in the first place because there were some cute girls who signed up for it!

I appreciate your help in clearing my good name.

Sincerely,

Sid Straw

Sid Straw

2748 Palmeyer Street Apt. 230
Baltimore, Maryland 21201

Dear Ms. Portino:

I am in receipt of your letter in which you informed me that New Solutions Software has rescinded its offer of employment to me. I am saddened, disappointed and confused by this rather abrupt decision. I had been looking forward to taking the marketing team into a new and exciting direction.

I would appreciate it if you would call me at your convenience to discuss the revocation of your offer.

Thank you.

Sincerely,

Sid Straw

2748 Palmeyer Street Apt. 230
Baltimore, Maryland 21201

Dear Mr. Spellman:

ARE YOU GIVING MY LETTERS TO HEATHER, OR NOT?

At the very least, I deserve an answer to that simple, straightforward question.

Sincerely,

Sid Straw

Dear Ms. Portino:

Thank you for your telephone call earlier today. Would it be possible for you to send me a copy of the references and the background investigation report that the company obtained? I suspect they may be erroneous.

Thank you.

Very truly yours,

Sid Straw

2748 Palmeyer Street Apt. 230
Baltimore, Maryland 21201

Dear Agent Friedlander:

There was absolutely no reason for you to interrogate my mother. You scared the life out of her. Yes, her maiden name was DeCastro, but that's *Italian*, not *Cuban*. She's not related in any way to Fidel Castro, as the fact that they have different last names would suggest. In any event, I assure you that my mother is an American through and through. Her only crime is being a bad cook, which I believe is outside your agency's jurisdiction.

I hope you and your colleagues will be more professional in the future.

Sincerely,
Sid Straw

2748 Palmeyer Street Apt. 230
Baltimore, Maryland 21201

Dear Ms. Portino:

Thank you for forwarding a copy of my references and my background investigation report. As I suspected, they are erroneous (or, at least, misleading).

First, I am not now, nor have I ever been, a Communist. I didn't even know there WERE Communists anymore.

Second, the restraining orders are a terrible, terrible mistake. They were obtained in Los Angeles while I was in Baltimore, as I have been for most of the past 20 years. I was not present at the hearings where the restraining orders were granted. As such, I had no opportunity to defend myself or to tell the judges my side of the story. It is a terrible, terrible misunderstanding.

Third, I did not engage in "wildly inappropriate" conduct while employed by Empire Software. I am afraid that there has been a terrible misunderstanding there as well.

I hope you will reconsider your decision to rescind my job offer. I truly believe I can help take the marketing team into the future!

Sincerely,

Sid Straw

═══ Sid Straw ═══
2748 Palmeyer Street Apt. 230
Baltimore, Maryland 21201

Dear *[InsertName]:*

I was wondering whether the *[insert title]* position is still available. I would like to be considered again and truly believe I can help lead your marketing team into the future!

I look forward to hearing from you soon.

Sincerely,

Sid Straw

2748 Palmeyer Street Apt. 230
Baltimore, Maryland 21201

Dear Sir or Madam:

I would like to reapply for unemployment compensation. Thank you.

Sincerely,

Sid Straw

═══ Sid Straw ═══

2748 Palmeyer Street Apt. 230
Baltimore, Maryland 21201

To the Baltimore Union Mission:

I recently sent you a check for $100. Unfortunately, my bank informs me that you have already cashed the check. Because of unforeseen circumstances, I am afraid that I must ask you to return the money to me as soon as possible. Please send a check to the above address as soon as possible. Thank you.

Sincerely,
Sid Straw

Flower Land

Dear Mom,
I am very soory about the incident with the CIA.
Especially what they said about your cooking.
Love,
Ted

═══ Sid Straw ═══

2748 Palmeyer Street Apt. 230
Baltimore, Maryland 21201

To Whom It May Concern:

Please cancel my cable television services. I am afraid I can no longer afford them.

Thank you.

Sincerely,

Sid Straw

Dear Ms. Portino:

It was a political science class I took in college!

Sincerely,

Sid Straw

Dear Dr. Katz:

I do not know if you will remember me or not. I was a student of yours about 20 years ago. I took a class you taught entitled "The Relevance of Lenin and Marx in Late Twentieth Century America." My paper was entitled "Lenin versus the Middle Class Social Self- Consciousness." Perhaps you will recall it: you gave me a B on it.

In any event, I would like to ask a favor. Would you mind writing a note to Ann Portino at New Solutions Software explaining that your class did not *promote* communism, but merely *discussed* and *analyzed* it? Your note would be most helpful in my efforts to secure employment.

Thank you.

Sincerely,

Sid Straw

2748 Palmeyer Street Apt. 230
Baltimore, Maryland 21201

Dear Agent Friedlander,

I do not know where you have obtained your information, but I have never threatened to strangle my sister-in-law, and I have never claimed to have given Sharon Stone a wedgie in high school. I didn't even go to high school with Sharon Stone. You're thinking of Dave Lambert, not me!

Sincerely,

Sid Straw

Sid Straw

2748 Palmeyer Street Apt. 230
Baltimore, Maryland 21201

Dear Dr. Katz:

I received your note in today's mail. I believe you are mistaken: I wasn't the one who fell asleep in class; YOU were. Remember someone wrote on the blackboard "JUST A LITTLE KATZ NAP?" Remember?

In any event, could you send a short note to Ann Portino at New Solutions Software? It would be most appreciated.

Sincerely,

Sid Straw

══ Sid Straw ══

2748 Palmeyer Street Apt. 230
Baltimore, Maryland 21201

Dear Mom,
I said I was sorry!
Love,
Sid

Dear Dave,

    I am SO sorry!

    Please apologize to Sarah and the kids for me. I am sure it was a very trying experience for all of them.

    Sincerely,

    Sid

    P.S. To make up for all the trouble I've inadvertently caused, I've written a little story for your kids called "Fred Smells." I hope they enjoy it!

Dear Agent Friedlander:

I have just learned that not only have you interrogated my friend Dave Lambert and his family, but now you have subpoenaed records from the FLORIST that I use. You are going too far. I have never used the "alias" of "Ted." Those were typographical errors made by the florist!!!

Please stop this nonsense.

Sincerely,

Sid Straw

$$=== \quad \text{Sid Straw} \quad ===$$

2748 Palmeyer Street Apt. 230
Baltimore, Maryland 21201

Dear Dr. Katz:

I just received your note.

I was NOT the person who wrote "JUST A LITTLE KATZ NAP" on the blackboard.

Sincerely,

Sid Straw

Dear Agent Friedlander:

I am begging you to stop harassing my mother. She is a good woman, and your suggestion that she has had a romantic relationship with Ted Monaghan is outrageous.

Once again, I ask you to please stop this nonsense.

Thank you.

Sincerely,

Sid Straw

2748 Palmeyer Street Apt. 230
Baltimore, Maryland 21201

Dear Dave,

I just received your letter. Of course I remember that one of your sons is named Fred. I just don't understand why he would be so upset. If you read the story, you would see that when I said "Fred smells," I meant that he uses his nose to smell things, not that he stinks. In fact, I think it's pretty clear in the story. Please go back and reread it.

Sincerely,

Sid Straw

═══ Sid Straw ═══
2748 Palmeyer Street Apt. 230
Baltimore, Maryland 21201

Dear Agent Friedlander:

Yes, I wrote "Fred Smells." But I don't understand why Dave Lambert would share it with you, or why you would find it the least bit interesting. It's a children's story, that's all. Although the narrator conducts tests in his cellar, I assure you that I don't conduct tests in my cellar—nor could I since I don't have a cellar! And although the narrator blindfolds his friend, I assure you that I have never done that.

Sincerely,
Sid Straw

Sid Straw

2748 Palmeyer Street Apt. 230
Baltimore, Maryland 21201

Dear Dr. Katz:

I don't care what Dave Lambert told you: I was NOT the person who wrote "JUST A LITTLE KATZ NAP" on the blackboard. And I'm not going to tell you who did! It's been 20 years, for godssakes! Who cares anymore?

Sincerely,

Sid Straw

P.S. Want to know who wrote that anonymous letter to *The Daily Bruin* calling you incompetent and a "disgrace to academia"? DAVE LAMBERT, that's who!

Dear Ms. Portino:

Thank you for forwarding a copy of the note you received from Dr. Katz. Obviously, he's a sad and disturbed man. In any event, I hope you will keep me in mind for any positions that become available at New Solutions.

Sincerely,

Sid Straw

Sid Straw

2748 Palmeyer Street Apt. 230
Baltimore, Maryland 21201

To the Unemployment Commission:

I'm afraid there was a typographical error on my unemployment check this week. It was made out to "Sad Striw" instead of "Sid Straw." (Apparently, the "i" and the "a" were transposed.) I don't know how your records could indicate that my name is "Sad." I'd appreciate it if you could correct this error on future checks. (I doubt there will be many more future checks as I have three job interviews next week!)

Thank you for taking care of this problem.

Sincerely,

Sid Straw

Sid Straw

2748 Palmeyer Street Apt. 230
Baltimore, Maryland 21201

To Whom It May Concern:

Please let this letter serve as my notice that I will be vacating my apartment at the end of the month.

Any future correspondence should be sent to me in care of my parents, Alexander and Helen Straw, at the following address:

Mr. Sid Straw
18 Pony Place
Towson, Maryland 21294

Thank you.
Sincerely,
Sid Straw

=== Sid Straw ===

2748 Palmeyer Street Apt. 230
Baltimore, Maryland 21201

To the United States Post Office:

Please forward my mail to the following address:
Mr. Sid Straw
c/o Alexander and Helen Straw
18 Pony Place
Towson, Maryland 21294

Thank you.
Sincerely,
Sid Straw

SID STRAW
18 PONY PLACE
TOWSON, MARYLAND 21294

To Whom It May Concern:

This letter is sent to inform you of my change of address.
Please send my copies of *Sports Illustrated* to the above address.

Thank you.

Sincerely,

Sid Straw

To Whom It May Concern:

This letter is sent to inform you of my change of address. Please send my copies of *Entertainment Weekly* to the above address.

Thank you.

Sincerely,

Sid Straw

SID STRAW
18 PONY PLACE
TOWSON, MARYLAND 21294

To Whom It May Concern:

This letter is sent to inform you of my change of address. Please send my copies of *People* to the above address.

Thank you.

Sincerely,

Sid Straw

SID STRAW
18 PONY PLACE
TOWSON, MARYLAND 21294

To Whom It May Concern:

    This letter is sent to inform you of my change of address. Please send my copies of *US* to the above address.

    Thank you.

    Sincerely,

    Sid Straw

To Whom It May Concern:

This letter is sent to inform you of my change of address. Please send my copies of *Playboy* to the above address.

Thank you.

Sincerely,

Sid Straw

SID STRAW
18 PONY PLACE
TOWSON, MARYLAND 21294

To Whom It May Concern:

This letter is sent to inform you of my change of address. Please send my copies of *Penthouse* to the above address.

Thank you.

Sincerely,

Sid Straw

To Whom It May Concern:

This letter is sent to inform you of my change of address.

Please send my copies of *Big Boobs* to the above address. I am also enclosing a dozen adhesive labels that indicate that your packages are being sent from the American Cancer Society. I would appreciate it if you would affix these labels to the envelopes before sending them to the above address.

Sincerely,

Sid Straw

Dear Mrs. Kramer:

I am in receipt of your letter sent on behalf of the Maryland Unemployment Commission. I assure you that "Sad Striw" is not an alias, and I am not trying to defraud the Commission. I have never gone by the name "Sad Striw." It was merely a typographical error on my unemployment check. I did not understand that cashing a check made out to "Sad Striw" would be problematic. It will not happen again.

Sincerely,

Sid Straw (not "Sad Striw")

SID STRAW
18 PONY PLACE
TOWSON, MARYLAND 21294

Dear Heather,

Just a note to give you my new address. I was unable to find any work and, as a result, have had to move into my parents' home. Hopefully, it'll only be temporary. Nevertheless, it's pretty humiliating. It's only a matter of time before the neighborhood kids start ringing the doorbell: "Mrs. Straw, can Sid come out and play?" (There is an up-side: I imagine I'll be one of the first kids picked for every team! Hooray for me!) Worse, there is a great deal of tension between my parents and their next-door neighbors, the Monaghans.

I don't want to go into too much detail about how pathetic it is to be living with my parents again; I'm afraid it might make me start crying. I'll tell you this though: Tom's wife's birthday is next week, and I might have to borrow money from my parents to get her a gift! I'm SERIOUS!

Take care.

Eat Wheaties!

Sid Straw

P.S. HELP!

SID STRAW
18 PONY PLACE
TOWSON, MARYLAND 21294

Dear Heather,

I just sent you a note yesterday and had a horrible thought—it might have seemed that I was asking you to lend me some money. I most certainly was NOT doing that. I sincerely apologize if it came across that way.

Eat Wheaties!

Sid Straw

SID STRAW
18 PONY PLACE
TOWSON, MARYLAND 21294

Dear Heather,
MY MOTHER TRIED TO TUCK ME IN LAST NIGHT!
HELP!
Eat Wheaties!
Sid Straw

SID STRAW
18 PONY PLACE
TOWSON, MARYLAND 21294

Dear Heather,

Today I cut the lawn and took out the garbage. I can't wait to get my allowance! I'm thinking about using it to buy some new Hot Wheels and the loop-the-loop track!

Eat Wheaties!

Sid Straw

P.S. HELP!

Janet,
Happy Birthday!
I hope you like the belt—I did the
beadwork myself.

Sid

SID STRAW
18 PONY PLACE
TOWSON, MARYLAND 21294

Dear Tom,

I was NOT trying to be funny. I'm broke. Besides, if you look in the new *People* magazine, you'll see that all of the stars are wearing beaded belts these days!

Sid

SID STRAW
18 PONY PLACE
TOWSON, MARYLAND 21294

Dear *[InsertName],*

I am writing to inquire about employment opportunities with your company. As you will see from the enclosed resume, I have worked in the computer field for nearly two decades. I believe my experience and my enthusiasm can help take the company into the future!

I look forward to hearing from you soon.

Sincerely,

Sid Straw

OBJECTIVE:

To help take a computer software entity into the future

EDUCATION:

University of California at Los Angeles

(B.A., Major-English, Minor-Computer Sciences)

EMPLOYMENT:

Consultant, present

Empire Software, nine years

Regional Vice President

Assistant Vice President

Regional Manager

Compu-Tech Software, four years

Regional Manager

Salesperson

Compu-Craft Computers, six years

Salesperson

HOBBIES:

Reading, sports, computers.

SID STRAW
18 PONY PLACE
TOWSON, MARYLAND 21294

Dear Heather,

I still haven't found the right job yet, but I'm in no hurry. It's probably not all that different from your career. You don't want to say "yes" to every script that they throw in front of you; you want to wait for the "right" one. It's just a matter of time, I'm sure.

While I've got some time on my hands, I've started playing softball in a coed league here in town. So far, so good. I'm on a team called "the Lemonheads" (named after the candy). I don't know anyone on the team but they all seem like nice people. I'm playing rightfield. We won our first game 10-6, then went out for pizza and beer afterwards. It's always nice to make new friends.

I hope all is well with you these days.

Take care.

Eat Wheaties!

Sid Straw

P.S. I still haven't been able to find Tracy Swid's address or phone number. The alumni office's information is *completely* outdated. They say she's living in Philadelphia, but when I tried the number they gave me, the person who answered had never heard of Tracy. You wouldn't know how to reach her, would you?

Dear Mr. Spellman:

    I haven't heard from Heather recently.

    Would you please confirm that you're forwarding my notes to her?

    Thanks,

    Sid Straw

SID STRAW
18 PONY PLACE
TOWSON, MARYLAND 21294

Dear Heather,

I woke up this morning, watched television and read the newspaper. And as I was turning the pages, I noticed the date at the top of the page and realized that today is my birthday. Today is my 42nd birthday, and not only has everyone else forgotten, but I'd forgotten, too.

I'm 42 years old now.

I have no friends to speak of.

I live with my parents.

They don't even have cable television.

I used to be happy. You remember me, Heather. You remember how happy I was, don't you? Don't you?

Sid Straw

SID STRAW
18 PONY PLACE
TOWSON, MARYLAND 21294

Dear Heather,

I know you're not reading these letters. I know they're not even reaching you. I know that. I do.

If anyone ever asks me, I tell them I knew a movie star once. I knew her before she was a movie star, before I even had a sense that she might someday become a movie star, when she was just some cute, funny girl I'd talk to every once in a while. And I liked her before she became a movie star. She was a good and decent and honest person, and when I see her on TV or read about her in a magazine now, I can tell that she's still a good and decent and honest person. I don't care how good of an actress she is, she still has that same look in her eyes and the same twist of a smile that tells me that she really is the same good and decent and honest person whom I knew once. And if she's still good and decent and honest, then maybe all of these movie stars are good and decent and honest, too, because that's what I want them to be. George Clooney and Meryl Streep and Nicole Kidman and Tom Cruise and Catherine Zeta-Jones, maybe they're all good and decent and honest, too, because surely there were people who knew and liked them before they became stars, right? Maybe all of them are just normal people, just like the girl I knew in college. Maybe they're just like the rest of us, in a way. And if they can succeed and be happy, maybe I can do the same, right? And maybe every once in a while, when they have a quiet moment and close their eyes, they think of the rest of us. And maybe, just maybe, they root for us the same way we root for them. Maybe they're rooting for me right now.

So I know you're not reading these letters, Heather. I know that the same way I know that the sky is blue, that ice is cold, that the sun will struggle up in the morning and the world will keep turning. But I'm going to keep writing these letters anyway, if you don't mind. I'm afraid of what will happen if I stop. I'm afraid I'll literally stop breathing. These letters are all I have these days. These letters and the dim hope that a girl I barely knew in college is thinking of me and praying for me.

Sid Straw

SID STRAW
18 PONY PLACE
TOWSON, MARYLAND 21294

To the Baltimore Union Mission:

I am in receipt of your recent letter, which was forwarded to my new address. I completely understand your position. I hope you understand my position as well; I'm afraid I've been going through a very difficult time both personally and financially. How about if we just split it down the middle and you return $50 to me? That makes sense, don't you think?

Keep up the good work. I will look forward to hearing from you soon.

Sincerely,

Sid Straw

Dear Mrs. Kramer:

THERE IS NO SUCH PERSON AS "SAD STRIW"! NOT NOW, NOT EVER!

Sincerely,

Sid Straw (not "Sad Striw")

SID STRAW
18 PONY PLACE
TOWSON, MARYLAND 21294

Dear Mrs. Kramer:

Please stop sending letters to "Sad Striw." THERE IS NO SUCH PERSON. Really. I swear.

Sincerely,

Sid Straw

SID STRAW
18 PONY PLACE
TOWSON, MARYLAND 21294

Dear Mrs. Kramer:
      Please stop faxing me letters.
      Sincerely,
      Sid Straw

Dear Mrs. Kramer:

Thank you for your note regarding Sid Straw, who apparently cashed one of my unemployment checks. While I appreciate your suggestion, I have no interest in prosecuting Mr. Straw. I am curious about two things, however: 1) how did you find out about the restraining orders, and 2) who told you he was a Communist?

Sincerely,
Sad Striw

SID STRAW
18 PONY PLACE
TOWSON, MARYLAND 21294

To the American Cancer Society,

There appears to be a terrible mix-up. I have no idea how this could have happened. I agree that there is no humor to be found in this incident.

I am enclosing a donation of $50.00. I hope it will help in your efforts to rid the world of this terrible disease. Have you considered that the answer might be found in the oxygen molecule?

Sincerely,

Sid Straw

To Whom It May Concern:

The adhesive labels I sent you for my copies of *Big Boobs* were to be used for the sender, not the recipient, of the envelopes. The packages should indicate that they are sent *from* the American Cancer Society; they should not be sent *to* the American Cancer Society.

I would appreciate it if you would make that correction in the future.

Sincerely,
Sid Straw

SID STRAW
18 PONY PLACE
TOWSON, MARYLAND 21294

To the Baltimore Union Mission:

I don't mean to rush you, but I really need that $50 back. Thank you.

Sincerely,

Sid Straw

To the Baltimore Union Mission:

Thank you very much for the food delivery that you made to me and my family at my parents' home last night. It was very kind of you, but it was entirely unnecessary. While I have had a rough time of late, we are not in need of your assistance.

Thank you again. Keep up the good work.

Sincerely,

Sid Straw

Dad,

I apologize for what happened last night. I am sorry that you were embarrassed in front of the neighbors.

I have already written to the Baltimore Union Mission to let them know that there is no reason to deliver food to us.

Love,
Sid

SID STRAW
18 PONY PLACE
TOWSON, MARYLAND 21294

Dear Heather,

I just had a memory. I just had a memory about some-thing I'm certain I hadn't thought of in the past ten years, if not longer than that, and I had to write to you right away.

Do you remember that intramural volleyball team you and I were on freshman year? The name of our team was something silly like "Hot Girls and the Men Who Adore Them," and the only reason I played at all was because Tracy Swid was on the team and I was convinced that it was a good way to get to know her. I think the team was me, you, Tracy, Dave Lambert, Tommy Aimes, Cindy Calcaterra—those are the only ones I can remember right now. And I remember that we must have had the shortest team in the entire league—not one of us was over six feet tall.

Anyway, I remember that we signed up late, so we got put in the most competitive league. I remember we lost every single match, often by a large margin, but we always had fun and would go out for pizza and beer afterwards. Until the time we had to play a bunch of jocks from one of the fraternities. They were huge, and they were good athletes; I think some were on the football team. I remember that they were killing us, that we could hardly score a point, that they were spiking ball after ball. But what I also remember is that instead of being decent about beating us, they were horrible. They were making rude comments about what they wanted to do to you and Tracy and the other girls, and they were poking fun at all of the guys on our team.

Do you remember any of this?

Do you remember that we were a couple points away from losing the match? A couple points, and then we could all go out for beer and pizza? But then you called a timeout, and when we all gathered in a huddle you said, "Did all of you eat your Wheaties this morning? Because now's the time when they're going to kick in. Let's beat these jerks." Then you gave everyone instructions about what we were all supposed to do. And just before we went on the court, I remember you winking at me and whispering, "It works in the movies." But what happened next was incredible. It actually sends a chill down my spine just thinking about it again. We started playing like we'd never played before. I can picture Cindy setting the ball, I can picture Tommy spiking it. We started winning point after point. I remember you looking at me, opening your eyes wide and mouthing, "Oh my *God*" like you couldn't believe what was happening. A couple times we were one point away from losing the match, but somehow we'd end up staving off defeat—Dave would block a spike, or Tracy would dig a ball out just before it hit the floor—and then we'd win a few more points. It would make a much better story if we ended up winning, but we didn't. But we almost won, and it was far closer than it had any right to be. And *that* was when you started saying, "Eat Wheaties" whenever you said goodbye to people. *That's* what started it.

Do you remember any of this? Because I remember it all so clearly now.

And I'll tell you something else: things haven't been going too well for me lately, but I had my Wheaties this morning, and I feel them about to kick in.

Thanks, Heather! Whether you get this letter or not, you have my thanks.

Sid

SID STRAW
18 PONY PLACE
TOWSON, MARYLAND 21294

Dear Mr. Frankel:

I am sorry if my initial reaction to your job offer was less enthusiastic than you had expected. After having thought about it, I am pleased to accept your offer of a Salesperson position. I look forward to a long and mutually satisfying career at Spartina Software. While a Salesperson position is a step back for me, I assure you that you've just hired the best Salesperson you've ever had. I know it's just a matter of time before I'll be taking on some managerial duties and helping to lead the company into the future!

I look forward to seeing you on Monday morning for orientation.

Sincerely,
Sid Straw

SID STRAW
18 PONY PLACE
TOWSON, MARYLAND 21294

Dear Heather,

Great news—I got a new job at Spartina Software!

Other great news—I met a terrific girl at one of our softball games. Her name is Debra. She's got brown hair and green eyes, and she's a heck of a softball player, too. She's an angel, Heather, an absolute angel. Anyway, I'm having dinner with her on Thursday night. Keep your fingers crossed for me (except when shaving your legs, of course—that could be dangerous!).

Hope all is well with you these days.

Eat Wheaties!

Sid Straw

P.S. Assuming things work out with Debra and she accompanies me to the reunion (if I still go), I'd appreciate it if you wouldn't tell her about the restraining orders. Or how I was fired. Or the harassment charges. Or my children's story. Or my novel. (Actually, it might be best if you pretend you don't understand English!)

SAD STRIW
18 PONY PLACE
TOWSON, MARYLAND 21294

Dear Mrs. Kramer,

I regret to inform you that Sad Striw has died tragically.

Sincerely,
Mrs. Sad Striw

Dear Heather,

I've been out twice with Debra. She's a terrific girl. She's pretty, and she has a great sense of humor (meaning that she laughs at all my jokes). This could be the one.

Anyway, I need to get back to work.

Again, my apologies.

Eat Wheaties!

Sid Straw

P.S. Have you signed up for the reunion events yet?

Dear Mrs. Kramer,
    It was a hunting accident.
    Sincerely,
    Mrs. Sad Striw

Dear Mom and Dad,

I have no idea who ordered those magazines! It must be a practical joke someone in the neighborhood is playing.

Love,

Sid

SID STRAW
18 PONY PLACE
TOWSON, MARYLAND 21294

Dear Agent Friedlander:

No, I'm not trying to "flee." If I were trying to flee, would I give the post office "change of address" forms? I'd have to be the stupidest criminal in the world, and I'm certainly not that stupid. Or a criminal.

Now, will you kindly leave me and my family alone?

Sincerely,

Sid Straw

Dear Mr. Haring:

Thank you for your interest in publishing an article about the disappearance of my husband's corpse in *The Los Angeles Times*.

I am afraid I cannot cooperate with you on your story. Please let me and the children grieve with dignity. If you really feel you must write about this matter, perhaps you should contact Frank Riceborough or Henry Callahan. They were the people who were hunting with my husband when he was "accidentally" shot.

Sincerely,

Mrs. Sad Striw

Dear Mr. Monaghan,

I hope you are feeling better.

I am sure you will be out of the hospital in no time at all!

Please understand that I did not tell my father that you were sending pornographic magazines to our home.

In any event, I hope these chocolates will cheer you up.

Sincerely,

Sid Straw

P.S. It appears that you mistakenly included a photograph of yourself sporting a black eye. It was a mistake, wasn't it?

Dear Mr. Fisk:

Thank you for your note. I am pleased to hear you are a member in good standing of the Maryland State Bar once again. I am also pleased that you will be able to assist my father with the assault charges that were brought against him following his fistfight with Ted Monaghan. I assure you that it was part of a terrible misunderstanding.

I will keep you in mind should I ever have the need for legal advice myself.

Sincerely,

Sid Straw

Dear Mr. Monaghan,

I was very disturbed by the message you left on my answering machine just moments ago. There is no reason to curse like that.

How was I supposed to know you were diabetic?

Sincerely,

Sid Straw

P.S. By the way, although I may not have known that you were a diabetic, *you* certainly did. So why on earth would you eat the chocolates in the first place?! The box was clearly marked "chocolates."

Dear Mr. Fisk:

I am writing to follow up on our telephone conversation this morning.

My father and I will meet you at your office at 4:00 p.m. next Tuesday to discuss our current legal needs. I am pleased to hear that you will allow me to sign over a check from the Maryland Unemployment Commission to pay for your services.

Sincerely,

Sid Straw

Dear Mr. Haring:

I am enclosing a photograph of my beloved Sad for your upcoming story in *The Los Angeles Times*. I hope you will excuse the fact that he has a black eye in the photograph, but it was the only photograph of him I could bear to part with. Hopefully, your readers will be able to help find his corpse so we can give him a proper burial. Please make sure to note that he was last seen hunting in California with his good friends Frank Riceborough and Henry Callahan. Please make sure they also understand that there may have been an argument about payment for a shipment of marijuana. Or cocaine. Whichever the really bad one is.

Very truly yours,

Mrs. Sad Striw

SID STRAW
18 PONY PLACE
TOWSON, MARYLAND 21294

Dear Mr. Buckner:

I have met with my new attorney. He informs me that it was unlawful of you to require me to pay $320.00 when I never retained you. Accordingly, unless you return the $320.00 to me within two weeks of the date of this letter, we will initiate a lawsuit against you. Assuming for the sake of argument that you will only need to invest three hours of your time to defend the lawsuit, it will cost you approximately $1,000.00 of your time if you choose to fight this.

I will look forward to your response.

Sincerely,

Sid Straw

Dear Mr Fisk:

    Thank you for your excellent work in convincing the district attorney's office to dismiss all charges against my father. You were certainly right when you said that this was a "crime of passion."

    Sincerely,

    Sid Straw

SID STRAW
18 PONY PLACE
TOWSON, MARYLAND 21294

Dear Heather,

You'll never believe this. At dinner last night, Debra informed me that her company is transferring her. You'll never guess where they are transferring her—Los Angeles! I can't believe it. We haven't been dating long enough for me to ask her to stay: it's only been a month. At the same time, I'll be devastated if she leaves. I don't know what, if anything, to do.

I actually stayed up last night and wrote her a poem. This is it:

The Stars and Me
by Sid Straw

Watch the midnight stars and moan,
In four hours or so, they'll leave you alone.
They're only stars, they will not miss you,
They cannot hope or dream to kiss you.

They can never take your hands and dance,
Watch you walk into a room in your capri pants,
Listen to you sing (wobbly, off-key),
That's the difference between the stars and me.
The oceans and seas could turn to ink,
And I would find something else to drink.
Air to gas, or fire, or coal.
I would find a way to breathe, I know.

But if you were to pack your bags and leave,
I'd have to teach my heart to beat.
Tell it how to get through each day.
Lie to it, say you'll come back someday.
The tall boats that could hasten your flight,
They all set their course by the stars at night.
Somehow, perhaps, I could make them realign,
So the port where you land will always be mine.

What do you think? Should I give it to her? Will she find it sweet and romantic—or will it scare her? Let me know. I value your opinion.

I hope all is well with you.

Eat Wheaties!

Sid Straw

P.S. She likes to wear capri pants. Hence, the line about the capri pants.

SID STRAW
18 PONY PLACE
TOWSON, MARYLAND 21294

Dear Mr. Buckner:

Thank you for your check in the amount of $320.00.

I am pleased we were able to resolve this matter without the need for messy litigation.

Sincerely,

Sid Straw

SID STRAW
18 PONY PLACE
TOWSON, MARYLAND 21294

Dear Mr. Fisk:
   Enclosed please find a check for $60.00.
   Thank you for your sound legal advice.
   Sincerely,
   Sid Straw

SID STRAW
18 PONY PLACE
TOWSON, MARYLAND 21294

Dear Agent Friedlander:

Murder? I don't know anything about any murder. Now that I think of it, I do remember Frank Riceborough and Henry Callahan saying something about a corpse and a dispute over some drug money, but I really didn't think much of it. Maybe you should interrogate them—and soon!

Sincerely,

Sid Straw

P.S. Why is the CIA investigating this? Isn't this out of the CIA's jurisdiction?

P.P.S. You didn't hear this from me, but I believe both Mr. Riceborough and Mr. Callahan were in Dallas in November 1963. Coincidence?

SID STRAW
18 PONY PLACE
TOWSON, MARYLAND 21294

Dear Heather,

Debra leaves for L.A. in two days. I didn't give her the poem after all. I'm going to miss her.

Anyway, she doesn't know a soul out there. Maybe you could give her a call sometime for lunch or dinner. She's a great girl. I think you two would really hit it off.

Thanks.

Eat Wheaties!

Sid Straw

Dear Ms. Portino,

As you will recall, several months ago you offered me a position with New Solutions, only to withdraw your offer after conducting a background check.

I have retained an attorney, who has informed me that the background check you conducted violated federal law. Specifically, if an employer wishes to conduct a background check of an applicant, the Fair Credit Reporting Act requires the employer to first obtain the applicant's express written permission. At no time did you ever get my express written permission to conduct a background check.

Because of your violation of the Fair Credit Reporting Act, I was unemployed for several months and suffered tremendous embarrassment and humiliation. At this time, my lawyer and I are prepared to file suit if we cannot resolve this matter amicably. If the company would like to make an offer to resolve this matter, please do so within the next two weeks.

Sincerely,
Sid Straw

Dear Ms. Portino,

I am pleased we have been able to resolve this matter amicably without the need for litigation. Please forward the settlement agreement and the $30,000.00 settlement check to me as soon as possible.

Sincerely,

Sid Straw

Dear Mr. Fisk:

Enclosed please find a check for $3,000.00.

Thank you for your sound legal advice.

Sincerely,

Sid Straw

SID STRAW
18 PONY PLACE
TOWSON, MARYLAND 21294

Dear Mr. Callahan:

I have no idea what you're talking about.
Sincerely,
Sid Straw

Dear Mr. Riceborough:

I have no idea what you're talking about.

Sincerely,

Sid Straw

SID STRAW
18 PONY PLACE
TOWSON, MARYLAND 21294

Dear Bob:

I hope this letter finds you well.

It has come to my attention that you provided false information to a number of prospective employers when they called Empire Software for a reference check. As you may know, this is known as "defamation" in the legal world. I would hate for us to get involved in nasty litigation about this matter, particularly since such litigation may require me to disclose information about your relationship with Cyndi in Human Resources. If you have any interest in trying to resolve our dispute in a less public manner, please let me know.

Sincerely,

Sid Straw

SID STRAW
18 PONY PLACE
TOWSON, MARYLAND 21294

Dear Bob:

I am pleased we were able to resolve this matter so swiftly.

Thank you for overnighting the $25,000.00 settlement check to me. Of course, you can count on me to adhere to the terms of the confidentiality agreement you drafted.

Sincerely,

Sid Straw

SID STRAW
18 PONY PLACE
TOWSON, MARYLAND 21294

Dear Mr. Fisk:

Thank you for your sound legal advice.
Enclosed is a check for $2,500.
Sincerely,
Sid Straw

World of Flowers

Debra—
I miss you.
Love,
Sid

SID STRAW
18 PONY PLACE
TOWSON, MARYLAND 21294

Dear Heather,

I'm going to be in Los Angeles next weekend to visit Debra.

Any chance you'll have some free time when we could get together?

Let me know.

Eat Wheaties!

Sid Straw

World of Flowers

Debra —
I'm sorry that you thought I was coming on too
strong when I signed my last card "Love, Sid."
Looking forward to seeing you this weekend.
Love,
Sid

SID STRAW
18 PONY PLACE
TOWSON, MARYLAND 21294

To Whom It May Concern:

Enclosed please find a check for two airline tickets I purchased from Baltimore, Maryland to Florence, Italy.

I would appreciate it if you would send them via overnight delivery as they are a gift.

Thank you.

Sincerely,

Sid Straw

SID STRAW
18 PONY PLACE
TOWSON, MARYLAND 21294

To the Baltimore Union Mission:

    Enclosed please find a check for $5,000.

    Keep up the good work.

    Sincerely,

    Sid Straw

Dear Heather,

I'm writing this letter from a plane headed toward L.A. I swear, the average age of the passengers on this flight is 18. Months, not years. There must be 50 babies on this flight, and they're all screaming. It's like some special Pampers promotion. There are two babies behind me, one next to me, and one in front of me. I am NOT kidding. I have no idea how I'm going to put up with this for five minutes, let alone five hours. Pray for me, will you?

I have to admit I'm a little nervous about seeing Debra. I'm sure everything will be terrific once we see each other, but I keep wondering if it makes sense to date a girl who lives 2,000 miles away. Does it?

The baby next to me just got sick. The baby behind me is making a noise that sounds like "Dabba-mogga-goo! Dabba-mogga-goo!" (Just thought you'd want to know.)

Work's work. It's not very exciting, and most of the people I work with are at least 10 years younger than me. I don't know any of the bands they listen to. Worse, have you noticed that people in their twenties never "say" anything? They always "go" or are "like." Here's an honest-to-God, verbatim conversation at work the other day:

Cathy: So Stephanie goes, "Do you want to come over on Saturday night?"

T.J.: She's all like weird, isn't she?

Cathy: Uh-huh. So I go, "I don't think so." Then she goes, "Come on, it'll be like great." And I'm all, "Whatever"

T.J.: Dabba-mogga-goo! Dabba-mogga-goo!

You get the point.

There's now a whole plane full of babies chanting, "Dabba-mogga-goo! Dabba-mogga-goo!" It's an uprising! I'm frightened!

The movie's about to start, so I'd better end this letter before they turn the lights down—or before the babies take over the plane and hijack it to Disneyland.

Wish me luck with Debra this weekend.

Take care.

Eat Wheaties!

Sid Straw

P.S. I'll be moving out of my parents' home in a couple weeks. Please file that under "Good News." It's a pretty thin file, isn't it?

Dear Heather,

Sorry I didn't get a chance to catch up with you while I was in L.A. visiting Debra. I'm sure you were very busy.

In any event, I don't think I'll be in L.A. again before the reunion. Let's just say that I don't think Debra and I will be seeing each other anymore. You don't really know someone until you spend 24 hours with them, if you know what I mean (and I'll bet you do).

Hope all's well with you these days.

Eat Wheaties!

Sid Straw

P.S. Do you know if Tracy Swid is going to the reunion?

To Altimo Holding Company:

Enclosed please find a check for $18,000.00 as a deposit on my new townhouse in Federal Hill. I will look forward to closing on the property at the end of the month.

If you have any questions, please do not hesitate to call.

Sincerely,

Sid Straw

SID STRAW
2628 Federal Hill Road No. 202
Baltimore, Maryland 21201

To Whom It May Concern:

This letter is to inform you of my change of address. Please send my copies of *Sports Illustrated* to the above address.

Thank you.

Sincerely,

Sid Straw

SID STRAW
2628 Federal Hill Road No. 202
Baltimore, Maryland 21201

To Whom It May Concern:

This letter is to inform you of my change of address. Please send my copies of *Entertainment Weekly* to the above address.

Thank you.

Sincerely,

Sid Straw

To Whom It May Concern:

This letter is to inform you of my change of address. Please send my copies of *People* to the above address.

Thank you.

Sincerely,

Sid Straw

To Whom It May Concern:

This letter is to inform you of my change of address. Please send my copies of *US* to the above address.

Thank you.

Sincerely,

Sid Straw

To Whom It May Concern:

This letter is to inform you of my change of address. Please send my copies of *Playboy* to the above address.

Thank you.

Sincerely,

Sid Straw

To Whom It May Concern:

This letter is to inform you of my change of address. Please send my copies of *Penthouse* to the above address.

Thank you.

Sincerely,

Sid Straw

To Whom It May Concern:

This letter is to inform you of my change of address. Please send my copies of *Big Boobs* to the above address.

Thank you.

Sincerely,

Sid Straw

To the United States Post Office:
Please forward all of my mail to the address above.

Thank you.
Sincerely,
Sid Straw

SID STRAW
2628 Federal Hill Road No. 202
Baltimore, Maryland 21201

Mom and Dad,

Just a quick note to thank you for letting me stay with you the past several months. I know you never expected to have me under your roof again. I appreciate all your kindness.

The airline tickets are just a token of my gratitude. Florence is supposed to be beautiful this time of year. (I'm speaking of course of Florence, Italy, not Florence Henderson. Although I'm sure Florence Henderson is lovely this time of year, too).

Your loving son,
Sid

To the Editor,

I have two friends who would like to be added to your mailing list for the *Spanking Times* newsletter. Please add Frank Riceborough and Henry Callahan to your mailing list; their work addresses are enclosed. I am also enclosing an article they have co- written entitled "No More Living A Lie! Our Many Years As Cross- Dressing Bondage Queens." I hope you will find the article suitable for publication in an upcoming issue.

Thank you for your attention to this matter.

Sincerely,

Sad Striw

P.S. Now that I think of it, please add my friend Sam Haller at Empire Software to your list. The address is in your files.

To the Skylar Publishing Company:

Enclosed is a money order for $39.95. Please send the following books to my friend Frank Riceborough:

1) *Barely Legal Babysitters*
2) *Get on Your Knees, Slave!*
3) *Transvestite Love Boys Get Lost*

The money order includes shipping and handling charges.

Sad Striw

To the Skylar Publishing Company:

Enclosed is a money order for $52.75. Please send the following books to my friend Henry Callahan:

1) *Call Me Mommy!*
2) *Call Me Mommy (Part II)!*
3) *Hooter Attack*
4) *Fat Chicks Who Love to Lick*

The money order includes shipping and handling charges.

Sad Striw

Dear Mr. Callahan:
I have no idea what you're talking about.
Sincerely,
Sid Straw

Dear Mr. Riceborough:
I have no idea what you're talking about.
Sincerely,
Sid Straw

To the Video Stars Corporation:

I saw your advertisement in this month's issue of *Big Boobs* and wanted to order the following videos for my friend Frank Riceborough:

1) *Nasty Sluts Get Nastier!*
2) *Call Me Mommy (The Movie)!*
3) *Ass Party*

A money order is enclosed.

Sad Striw

To the Aaron Adult Toy Company:

I am responding to your ad in *Big Boobs*. Please send items No. 22863 (extra large) and 462B (flesh colored) to my friend Henry Callahan.

A money order, including shipping and handling, is enclosed.

Sad Striw

Dear Mr. Callahan:
    I am in receipt of your letter.
    Are you threatening me?!
    Sincerely,
    Sid Straw

Dear Mr. Riceborough:
    I am in receipt of your letter.
    Are you threatening me?!
    Sincerely,
    Sid Straw

2628 Federal Hill Road No. 202
Baltimore, Maryland 21201

Dear Mr. Callahan:

Enclosed please find a restraining order that I have obtained from the District Court of Baltimore City. As you will see, it requires you to stay at least 150 yards away from me at all times. It is a shame that your threatening letters made this necessary.

Sincerely,
Sid Straw

SID STRAW
2628 Federal Hill Road No. 202
Baltimore, Maryland 21201

Dear Mr. Riceborough:

Enclosed please find a restraining order that I have obtained from the District Court of Baltimore City. As you will see, it requires you to stay at least 150 yards away from me at all times. It is a shame that your threatening letters made this necessary.

Sincerely,

Sid Straw

2628 Federal Hill Road No. 202
Baltimore, Maryland 21201

Dear Mr. Fisk:

As always, thank you for your excellent work.
Enclosed please find a check for $500.
Sincerely,
Sid Straw

Dear Mr. Marsh,

Thank you for forwarding the social security checks to me and my children. They will be quite helpful during this sad and difficult time.

Sincerely,

Mrs. Sad Striw

Dear Jeanne,

I just heard about your engagement to Sam Haller. Congratulations!

I wish you both all of the best!

Sincerely,

Sid Straw

P.S. Please give my best to everyone at Empire, especially Cyndi in Human Resources!

Dear Messrs. Riceborough and Callahan:

I will dismiss my restraining orders if you will dismiss yours—and get me reinstated to the UCLA reunion committee. Deal?

Sincerely,
Sid Straw

Dear Dean Warren:

Thank you for your invitation to rejoin the Reunion Committee. I proudly and enthusiastically accept.

Yes, I am aware that the reunion committee has not made arrangements for the Sunday brunch. I will take care of that immediately.

Sincerely,

Sid Straw

Dear Mr. Fisk:

Thank you for your sound legal advice. As you suspected, both Mr. Callahan and Mr. Riceborough agreed to withdraw their restraining orders.

I am enclosing a check for $250 for your services. Again, my thanks.

Best wishes,

Sid Straw

• UCLA REUNION COMMITTEE •

Dear *[InsertName]:*

    I am chairperson for our UCLA reunion class. We are looking for a ballroom that would be able to accommodate approximately 2,000 for brunch the second Sunday in November.

    Please let me know as soon as possible whether you would be able to accommodate us.

    Very truly yours,

    Sid Straw

Dear Mr. Rollinson:

Yes, I am aware that it's awfully late to be looking for a restaurant for reunion weekend. That's exactly why I wrote to you.

Sincerely,

Sid Straw

Dear Mr. Callahan:

I understand from your website that your law firm has a relationship with several well-known restaurants in Los Angeles. Would you mind putting me in touch with several of them—I'm afraid we do not have a restaurant lined up for our Sunday brunch during reunion weekend.

Thank you for your help.

Sincerely,

Sid Straw

SID STRAW
2628 Federal Hill Road No. 202
Baltimore, Maryland 21201

Dear Ms. Tomberlin:

I was thrilled to receive your note. It had been so long, I'd completely forgotten that I'd even sent the first chapter of *Invisible Sam* to you! In any event, I'm pleased to learn that you enjoyed it and that Skylar Publishing Company might be interested in publishing it.

I have not worked on the book for a while, but should be able to send you several more chapters in a couple weeks.

Thank you again for your comments. I hope you will enjoy the rest of the book as much as you enjoyed the first chapter.

Sincerely,

Sid Straw

P.S. I deleted the first chapter from my computer. Would you mind sending a copy of it back to me so I can type it back in? Thanks.

SID STRAW
2628 Federal Hill Road No. 202
Baltimore, Maryland 21201

Dear Heather,

Check out this letter I just got from an editor at Skylar Publishing Company! Incredible!

Now all I have to do is write the rest of the book!

Eat Wheaties!

Sid Straw

P.S. Did you notice that every one of my sentences ends in an exclamation point! Well, it's true! See, it just happened again!

• UCLA REUNION COMMITTEE •

Dear Mr. Steele:

    This letter is sent to confirm our telephone conversation regarding Sunday brunch at the reunion. I will forward a check shortly.

    Sincerely,
    Sid Straw

• UCLA REUNION COMMITTEE •

Dear Ms. Vitelli:

This letter is sent to confirm our telephone conversation regarding Sunday brunch at the reunion. I will forward a check shortly.

Sincerely,
Sid Straw

Dear Mr. Petrocelli:

This letter is sent to confirm our telephone conversation regarding Sunday brunch at the reunion. I will forward a check shortly.

Sincerely,

Sid Straw

Dear Heather,

I met the greatest girl yesterday. Get this: her name is Macy... and I met her at Macy's department store! What are the odds of that? It's like meeting someone named Exxon at an Exxon station, or someone named Blockbuster at a video store. (Feel free to make up your own. Go ahead. It's fun!)

Anyway, I was looking for a lamp for my living room, and I'm horrible at decorating. Being a single guy, I don't want anything too feminine. So I said to the saleswoman, "Do you have a boys' lamp section? You know, lamps with footballs or machine guns on them?" Macy was standing there, and she started laughing. Then she said to the saleswoman, "Would you mind pointing me toward the girls' lamps? I'm looking for something with Barbie dolls on it." Before you know it, we're helping each other pick out lamps, then going out for coffee. We're having dinner on Thursday night. Keep your fingers crossed for me.

Just as importantly, I've checked the records, and you haven't signed up for the reunion yet. Why are you procrastinating? Come on, sign up already! It'll be great fun.

I've got to run.

Take care.

Eat Wheaties!

Sid Straw

P.S. Here's something funny Macy told me. She said that if she ever has a daughter, she wants to name her Saturday. Why? BECAUSE EVERYONE LOVES SATURDAY. Pretty funny, don't you think?

• UCLA REUNION COMMITTEE •

Dear Classmate:

Believe it or not, the reunion is only a month away. We've already had a tremendous response. In fact, it looks like we might have the largest reunion group in UCLA history.

A number of you have been asking for details about the Sunday brunch. Well, we've been keeping our plans under wraps until now. Rather than spend a beautiful Sunday morning in a stuffy banquet room, we're going to have brunch outdoors ... under a tent ... on the beach in Malibu. Wait, it gets better! The brunch is going to be catered by... (we hope you're sitting down for this)... WOLFGANG PUCK! Hold on, it gets even better! Entertainment will be provided by ... (you'd better still be seated) ... world famous pianist and singer HARRY CONNICK, JR. (Our thanks to Henry Callahan of the Class of 1964 for helping us make arrangements with Messrs. Puck and Connick.)

We're looking forward to seeing everyone at the reunion. It should be a terrific weekend.

GO BRUINS!

Very truly yours,

Sid Straw

Chairperson

SID STRAW
2628 Federal Hill Road No. 202
Baltimore, Maryland 21201

Dear Dean Warren,
　　Thank you for your kind note. It was my pleasure.
　　Sincerely,
　　Sid Straw
　　Chairperson, Reunion Committee

Flower Land

Macy—
Has anyone told you that you're an angle?
-Sid

Flower Land

Mom —
Macy and I wanted to thank you for cooking such a lovely
dinner last night. We had a wonderful time.
Love,
Sid

Flower Land

Macy—
Get well soon.
Love,
Sid

Flower Land

Macy—
I think I love you! No, I'm positive I do!
Sid

SID STRAW
2628 Federal Hill Road No. 202
Baltimore, Maryland 21201

To Whom It May Concern:

Please cancel my subscription to *Playboy* effective immediately.

Sincerely,

Sid Straw

SID STRAW
2628 Federal Hill Road No. 202
Baltimore, Maryland 21201

To Whom It May Concern:

Please cancel my subscription to *Penthouse* effective immediately.

Sincerely,

Sid Straw

SID STRAW

2628 Federal Hill Road No. 202
Baltimore, Maryland 21201

To Whom It May Concern:

Please renew my subscription to *Big Boobs* for two more years. A check is enclosed.

Sincerely,

Sid Straw

Dear Kate,

Thank you for your sweet and touching note. I am so sorry to learn that things did not work out between you and your old boyfriend. However, I'm dating an absolutely wonderful girl now, and, as such, I don't have any interest in trying to "rekindle" our relationship. I wish you the best of luck with everything though.

Sincerely,

Sid Straw

P.S. Sorry to hear you lost your job. I'm sure you'll find something soon! I'll keep my fingers crossed for you.

Dear Janet,

I wanted to send you a quick note about two matters.

First, I wanted to tell you how excited I am for you and Tom about your pregnancy. It's terrific news, and I couldn't be happier for the two of you. You'll be great parents! (And I won't be half-bad as an uncle, I promise.)

Second, I wanted to make a much-belated apology for my behavior at your wedding. My conduct, though unintentional, was entirely inappropriate. I hope in time you'll come to forgive me. (In fact, if I ever get married, you are hereby invited to engage in whatever crazed and peculiar behavior you desire. Then we'll call it even.)

Again, congratulations about your wonderful news.

Love,

Sid

P.S. If you and Tom are looking for baby names, our parents liked "Sid." Just thought I'd throw that out for your consideration.

Dear Heather,

I know I haven't written in a while, but I wanted to share some great news: I got a promotion to Regional Manager. It's not much—I'm almost embarrassed to mention it—but now I feel like I can go to the reunion with my head held high.

Speaking of the reunion, it's only a couple weeks away and you still haven't signed up. Please sign up IMMEDIATELY. It'll be fun. I promise.

Eat Wheaties!

Sid Straw

P.S. Things with Macy are still going great! I really think you'd love her.

Dear Heather,

Thanks for your kind note. It was great to hear from you. You have no need to apologize for your agent's delay in forwarding my letters to you. I know how busy things get in Hollywood. (Actually, I don't "know" that at all; I just assume it's busy from everything everyone says.) No need to apologize for your lawyer, either.

There's no reason for you to be nervous about going back for the reunion next weekend. People are proud of you, Heather. I mean that sincerely. You're wrong in thinking that people will be laughing behind your back. Your success may be different from that of some of our classmates, but success is success. And, in your field, you're a TREMEN-DOUS success. But you know that already.

Also, thanks for the lovely picture of you and your family. I'm glad to hear you're enjoying married life. I'd love to meet your husband and your daughter—another reason why you should go to the reunion! (I promise not to tell them about Keith Steiner. I have no idea whatsoever how you could have dated that guy. He smelled like feet, or didn't you notice?) And I was thrilled to hear that your daughter got a kick out of "Fred Smells" when you read it to her! I guess it wasn't as terrible as I thought it was!

To answer your question, of course I remember the time you wrote "JUST A LITTLE KATZ NAP" on the blackboard in Dr. Katz's class. And who could forget the Watermelon Punch Party at Phi Mu sophomore year?! Even now, after all these years, I can't look at a watermelon without getting a little bit nauseated. You put WAY too much vodka in that punch! You girls were crazy—but that's why we all liked you!

Thanks also for your sweet comments about my promotion. I know it may not sound exciting to you—heck, it doesn't even sound exciting to ME—but it's nice to know that the people I work with appreciate me. (Yes, I will send you my new business card, as you requested. God only knows what you're going to do with it. Maybe you could slip it to Drew Barrymore, hint, hint.)

I need to get back to work. I'll drop you a note soon. In the meantime, I'll look forward to seeing you and your family at the reunion. DON'T CHICKEN OUT! We all love you and want to see you, so mark it on your calendar.

Eat Wheaties!

Your friend,

Sid Straw

P.S. I'm thrilled to hear that Tracy will be at the reunion. Maybe we could all go out for a drink. I'm sure Macy wouldn't object. The drinks, of course, are on me.

P.P.S. I can't believe you told Jay Leno about the time Dave Lambert gave Sharon Stone a wedgie when you were on *The Tonight Show* the other night!

Dear Janet,

Your apology was very kind, but entirely unnecessary. I was pleased to hear that Heather sent you a note to confirm that she in fact had autographed that photo for Tom's birthday. And it's just like her to invite you to join us all for dinner the next time she's in Baltimore. She's always been as sweet as pudding and twice as nice. But you're only allowed to have dinner with us if you agree to wear your beaded belt! Sounds like a fair deal to me. I worked hard on that! I cut one of my fingers!

Love,

Sid

Dear Heather,

Macy and I enjoyed seeing you and your family at the reunion last weekend. What a great time! Your husband is very charming, and your daughter is adorable. Macy wants to know if we can borrow her for a couple days! What's the going rate for something like that? Do we rent her by the day or by the week?

That was a hilarious story you told at brunch. I had no idea whatsoever that you had a bit of a crush on me back in college. I'm very flattered, to say the least.

Most importantly, I wanted to write to respond to your very kind offer. As much as Macy and I would love to spend Christmas with you and your family in Southern California, I'm afraid Macy had already told her parents we'll be spending it with them. In Detroit. That, I believe, ought to be proof enough that I'm in love. Maybe we can come out next year?

Again, it was great to sec you. And I promise I'll send you more of *Invisible Sam* if I ever get around to finishing it. I'm glad you enjoyed it so much, it's just so hard to find time to write!

Eat Wheaties!

Sid

P.S. Do you have any interest in co-chairing the next reunion with me? It's only five years away!

Dear Ms. Tomberlin,

Thank you for your comments regarding the different directions you envision taking the book after Chapter 1. While I appreciate your comments, I am pretty certain that I do not want to change the name of the book from *Invisible Sam* to *Insatiable Sam: The Man Who Loved Sluts*. In fact, maybe it'd be better if we just dropped this project altogether. I'm busy enough at work as it is.

Best wishes,
Sid Straw

Flower Land

Macy—
Those aren't my magazines! I SWEAR!
Ted

SID STRAW
2628 Federal Hill Road No. 202
Baltimore, Maryland 21201

Dear Heather,
    Can you do me a favor?
    —Sid

The End.

Acknowledgments

I'd like to acknowledge the friendship and patience of the following good people, all of whom have put up with my nonsense for far too long. They are, more or less alphabetically: Mike Andresino, Cecily Banks, Andy Bienstock, Kevin Bjerregaard, Sandra Bond, Reid Bowman, the Campbells, Mike Callahan, Claire Chanenchuk, the Cherofs, Milton Cummings, the DeAndreas, Andrea Dresdner, Eric Feinstein, Doug Fellman, Rich Hafets, Chris Hampton, Debbie Hennelly, Brent Houk, the Ianellos, my friends at Jackson Lewis, the Johns Hopkins University Class of 1984, Bert Johnson, Lisa Kluck, the Kuns, the Larias, Steve Lebau, Holly Levin, Ann Lloyd, the Longos, Lisa Mantone, Linda Mason, Sharon McConnell, the McGees, Nancy Miles, Susan Mullen, Mindy Novick, my friends at the law firm formerly known as Piper & Marbury, Carol Prescott, Bill Quinn, the Richardsons, Ann Rumsey, the Solitars, Teresa Siriani, Jon Spitz, Larry Stone, the University of Virginia School of Law Class of 1988, Gina Villetti, Pat Walsh, the Weymers, Cara Wilson and Michael Yockel. I can only hope that seeing your name in this book will make you smile and convince you to put up with me for another couple weeks. If not, I respectfully request that you cross your name out with a thick black magic marker. And, of course, special thanks to Heather Locklear, her management and her representatives, all of whom will hopefully get a bigger laugh out of this than anyone else.

About the Author

Michael Kun is the author of works of fiction and non-fiction. Among other recognitions, his novel *You Poor Monster* was a Barnes and Noble "Discover Great New Writers" selection and was chosen as "Book of the Year" by *Baltimore* magazine. His novel *The Locklear Letters* was adapted for a movie entitled *Eat Wheaties!* Starring Tony Hale, Elisha Cuthbert and Paul Walter Hauser and is being reprinted with that title in connection with the release of the movie.

About the Publisher

The Sager Group was founded in 1984. In 2012, it was chartered as a multimedia content brand, with the intention of empowering those who create art—an umbrella beneath which makers can pursue, and profit from, their craft directly, without gatekeepers. TSG publishes books; ministers to artists and provides modest grants; designs logos, products and packaging, and produces documentary, feature, and commercial films. By harnessing the means of production, The Sager Group helps artists help themselves. For more information, visit TheSagerGroup.net

More Books from
The Sager Group

Mandela was Late: Odd Things & Essays From the Seinfeld Writer Who Coined Yada, Yada and Made Spongeworthy a Compliment
by Peter Mehlman

#MeAsWell, A Novel
by Peter Mehlman

The Orphan's Daughter, A Novel
by Jan Cherubin

*Words to Repair the World:
Stories of Life, Humor and Everyday Miracles*
by Mike Levine

Miss Havilland, A Novel by Gay Daly

*Revenge of the Donut Boys:
True Stories of Lust, Fame, Survival and Multiple Personality*
By Mike Sager

Lifeboat No. 8: Surviving the Titanic
by Elizabeth Kaye

See our entire library at TheSagerGroup.net

THE SAGER GROUP

Artifex Te Adiuva

CPSIA information can be obtained
at www.ICGtesting.com
Printed in the USA
FSHW011953070221
78279FS